Let's Connect!

Goodreads: https://www.goodreads.com/author/
show/5854923
Facebook: https://www.facebook.com/
pgshriverwrites
Instagram: https://www.instagram/com/
pgshriverwrites

And remember, I love to hear from my fans. Write a
review for this book on Goodreads, Amazon, and
Barnes and Noble to help other readers connect with
this trilogy. Feel free to drop me a line or two at one
of the sites above, or email me at
author@pgshriver.com!

A Message From the Author

Thank you for reading The Gifted Ones Trilogy. I hope you enjoy reading it as much as I did writing it. I love the idea of superheroes, the sci-fi and fantasy of their worlds. As I move forward with this series, The Gifted Ones will hopefully join the graphic novel genre as they combat fictional worlds and villains in their modern day setting. I hope you will follow their journeys by signing up on pgshriver.com for news and updates.

In this crazy world of 2020, where heroes combat invisible threats to our lives every day, we could all use a little superhero break and some hopeful stories.

If you're interested in fantasy novels, visit my website to see a full list of my hardcovers. You'll also find my children's book series.

THE LOST PRINCE

BOOK

3

IN THE GIFTED ONES TRILOGY

P.G. SHRIVER

The Lost Prince by P.G. Shriver
The Lost Prince copyright © 2020 by P.G. Shriver
ISBN: 978-1-952726-05-7
Paperback Edition
Address comments and inquiries to the author:
author@pgshriver.com
Internet URL: https://www.pgshriver.com

ACKNOWLEDGEMENTS

Without fans of superhero fantasies, what would be the point of writing them? Fans deserve acknowledgment by authors. They're the people who keep writers writing— and working! With that in mind, I want to acknowledge a special young man. I don't know his name. I know he enjoys science fiction and fantasy because I met him at the Heart of Texas Comic Con one year. I was there with The Gifted Ones Trilogy, books one and two. He visited my booth, perused my books, and chatted with me about superheroes. I enjoyed our visit. When he left my booth, he turned back and with a glint of mischief said, "You should make one of the teenagers dress like a popular superhero in the next book."

As a writer, ideas come from many places and conversations. I would like to acknowledge this young "Batman" for his suggestion. You'll learn why when you begin reading this book.

I would also like to acknowledge my beta

reader, Mikayla Cantrell, for her suggestions and minor edits, as well as my husband and family for their encouragement and support.

Writing is a risky business today. It's as competitive today as it was twenty years ago to write a successful novel and subsequent series. That said, I would never give it up. No matter how hard it gets to bring my stories to the world, I will do so. Thank you, dear reader, for keeping me going!

Enjoy!

DEDICATION

This book is dedicated to the many heroes of 2020 who fight COVID 19 each day and those who self quarantine to distance themselves for the sake of keeping the rest of the world safe from this virus.

I would also like to dedicate this book to those who don't see the color of a person, but instead see the soul of that person, the heart from which they share with others, the good they shed upon our world. Even the lowliest person without home, job, or family has some good to offer this world; it's up to those of us who've found our way to light the path for others who are lost. And, it's those who lose sight of the good in people that fail to see their own good and what he or she has to offer others.

Having lived through many difficult, very personal, events in my own life— events that might have caused a different person to exit this world by their own hand— it's so necessary for us to lean on each other for survival, to love each other, and to help the strugglers.

I applaud those who are barely hanging on in this difficult time, still plugging away, still seeing the good, and trying to share that good with others.

We all were given a gift at birth to share with the world, to make a better world for mankind. It's so easy to fall into traps set by evildoers and follow the wrong path, but if we find our gifts, use our gifts, we can right our path and live a happy life. We will begin to see the good, again.

We can still make our world a better place.

There are so many "evils" in this world to combat, real life evils, and with that in mind, I acknowledge those who have found their gifts, those who use their gifts daily, and those who remain on their path to make this world a better place, and raise the positive vibrations of a suffering world.

May love, peace, and joy fill your hearts.

Crouched deep in the closet corner, black spandex clad knees shook with anticipation beneath his calloused hands. He couldn't believe he was hiding in a closet dressed in his Comic Con costume. If one of his friends saw him dressed this way now... he shook his head at the thought.

Only she could talk him into wearing this costume on a normal day. Of course, she was the only one who knew the truth about him.

She thought he was a real superhero.

Hmpf!

What did she know? She was only seven years old.

He could hear her soft footsteps approaching. He'd grown to love her so much this past six months. She was so innocent, so delicate, so happy— and in need of a big brother to protect her from the woes of this world. She'd become the little sister he never had the chance to know. Being her big brother made him feel strong, responsible, loved— in control. Nothing in *his life had allowed him those feelings before his new foster parents brought him here.*

As he squatted there, waiting for his sister to pull the door open, listening to her last few approaching steps, her high-pitched scream startled him from his hiding place. He burst from the closet, panic hidden beneath his masked face.

No!

No!

Not now!

His body shook with rage; his jaw muscles swelled as his teeth clenched. Every step became the longest sprint of his life, yet his stride seemed to slow down.

Her scream muffled, grew distant, silenced.

Nooooooooooo!

The word flourished deeply within and then rose in crescendo.

He wasn't going to make it.

Not this time.

By the time he made it to the other room, she would be dead, just like all of the other times.

He couldn't save her.

His sense of control was false.

He couldn't stop her death.

She thought he was a superhero.

The door creaked under his forceful push on the brass knob. She lay there, on the floor of her room, motionless, breathless, colorless. Flames licked the walls, circled the room, and concealed her from his view. From the center of the flames, he heard it, the laughter, the taunting, the voice of the faceless man.

Tears blurred the roaring flames as he relented to his grief. He couldn't fight it any longer. He wanted to give up.

When he finally consigned himself to the thought, another voice called to him, the voice of a girl, "Unite, Gifted Ones!" He peered through the watery flames for her face, for some hope, and there she was across from him in the hot spiraling whirlwind.

The constant drumming grew louder as Jamie woke from the nightmare, the Juniper tree he curled beneath little protection from the heavy drops bouncing and splashing into the already muddy ground. A puddle formed beneath his left side. Water trickled into his right ear through the needled branches above, a tiny waterfall winding its way over his auricle into the ear canal. He could feel the cool December rain building, seeping through the black spandex covering his body. The cape served well to protect him from the cold wind, but did nothing to keep the water away from his skin.

What Jamie wouldn't give for his own clothes and a rain slicker— better yet, a room with a warm bed.

Jamie's conspicuous costume drew too much attention when wandering the crowded streets, especially in small towns like this. He cringed at his foolish decision to flee his home without clothes and supplies.

On the plus side, the raindrops masked the hot tears trailing over the bridge of his nose.

Some hero!

Whenever the recurring nightmare brought him to the ledge of lunacy, a face loomed before him, her face. That sincere, hopeful look was the only image that refocused his thoughts.

Thinking about her, he rolled out from under the evergreen and sat upright, allowing the hard rain to wash dirt, leaves and wet needles from his costume.

Through the curtains of rushing water dripping down either side of his forward bent face, lightning flashed, followed by a roll of thunder so near him the ground vibrated his crossed ankles.

He squinted into the pouring rain and silently wished the seeking arms of lightning would find him, strike him, end this nightmare, but he knew that wasn't possible. He could never escape the endlessness of his lonely world, his life.

He'd tried.

In spite of the raindrops racing over his cheeks, he wiped at his hot tears.

They had left him in charge of her.

They had trusted him with her life.

Worse, he had trusted them... both of them... his foster parents who said they loved him, wanted to adopt him. Ha!

He closed his eyes to the images of the last time he'd seen the only other people he'd loved since his own family.

Never again would he trust anyone, love anyone.

Long strands of soft, brown hair framed a floating face full of hope. The wavering image pushed through his depression, grief, anger, warning him of his self-pity. "Don't give up, Jamie!" Her voice fell softly into his thoughts through the heavy drops. It was like she was there, right next to him, speaking directly to him. "You are a hero." Her translucent image smiled, a bittersweet lift at the corners of her mouth, the pain and loneliness in her eyes so familiar to him.

He scoffed, a harsh, ironic chuckle escaping his throat as he scanned the Comic Con costume he donned.

"Who are you?" Jamie begged of the brown-haired girl before sobs disarmed his sanity. He gritted his teeth against the drenching rain, then he released a thunderous scream.

When Jamie lowered his eyes from the gray, branch parted sky, he noticed a hooded figure in the distance dodging from one tree to another. Jamie squinted through sheets of rain as the figure moved closer, hiding and running. The rain gear looked like the ones he'd seen cops wear in the movies, but it was much shorter. Curling himself into a ball, he rolled beneath the Juniper, drew his cape around his body and tugged down a lower limb for camouflage.

"Shut up! Are you trying to get us killed?" Neka whispered harshly into the darkness. "You and that incessant whistling! Sheez!"

"I can't help it. I'm bored. How much longer do we have to wait here? I'm starving, too."

"Ugh! You're not the only one who's hungry! Just be quiet." She mouthed, turning an ear toward the barn door, listening intently for the gruff voice, trying to discern the muffled conversation through cracks in the old wood.

Steps.

Mumbles.

Deep voices.

A clearly stated fact, "I know I saw them over here, but there's no way into this old barn, as far as I can see. Boarded up all the way around." A young man's voice, probably not much older than two hiding in the barn.

He sounded so nice. And cute...

Neka wondered what he looked like. Her back pressed against the stall wall, she closed her eyes imagining his face.

Wouldn't it be nice to have a normal life? Date someone? Someone with a voice like that? She wondered, the face she created hovering in the darkness behind closed lids.

Her life had never been normal, but then, considering all she'd seen since her parents' disappearance, maybe normal wasn't such a great thing. Slowly she opened her eyes as if the one behind the muted steps on the other side of the wall might catch sight of her slight movement; her muscles stiffened as his shadow passed over a sunlit crack in the wood next to her.

An eye, the sliver of an eye. "Too dark to see anything in there. I tell ya', there's no way in. Been around it three times."

"A'ight. Let's call it in and get outta here. He ain't gonna be happy."

Who? Who's not going to be happy? The man who tore apart my family, maybe? Neka frowned.

Two car doors, a quiet engine, and tires crunching on gravel eased the tension in her muscles.

"Is it safe now?" The boy next to her whispered. There were days when his ignorance and arrogance made her want to punch him.

"Shh!" She peered angrily in his direction. She'd learned the silence seeming to wrap her in safety was the furthest from safe. Staying low, she crawled to a crack in the wall facing the gravel drive. She couldn't see the car, but something felt off. Intuition screamed from within, telling her to stay put, someone lurked beyond the wall, waiting for the two of them to slip up.

Was it intuition, or paranoia?

Following her intuition brought mistakes along the way and those mistakes cost her everything. One had cost her her parents. Her eyes stung with unshed tears as she returned to her spot through musty, dirty, dried hay— each swish surrounding her with the scent of old horse manure. Doubts filled her.

As annoying as the boy next to her was, she didn't want anything to happen to him. He was all that was left of her past— of her life.

She had to hold on to her brother, keep him safe.

She closed her eyes, inhaled the horse smell, and reached a calming, protective hand toward his knee but felt only dirt. Swearing out a sigh, she searched the darkness for his silhouette before rising to follow him.

"Stop!" She raced toward the worn wooden wall of the barn and reached for his arm, but the connection brought an electrically charged pain to her hand, up her forearm, her shoulder, her neck, her brain, then nothing... darkness... her body ripped into tiny pieces, atoms of charged energy exploding into the atmosphere. When she opened her eyes, she stood outside the barn facing wild, overgrown woods. Pressing her back against the barn wall, she shifted her eyes cautiously before breaking the stillness with motion.

What if that boy on the outside could still be lurking? Hmm! Might not be a bad thing. Wishful thinking!

Nothing happened.

The view over her left shoulder revealed nothing but cracks in the old barn wall, a rusting tin roof, empty bird nests in the eves, yet she shivered from head to toe.

Her extremities tingled with the anticipation of being caught.

She hated when Nashota became uncontrollable!

Her parents should have switched their names, but he was born after she was. No matter, to her the name Neka—meaning "wild goose"—fit his personality better!

Ugh!

She slipped along the barn wall, side stepped to the corner, and peeked around it.

Nothing.

Hopeful, anxious lungs deflated like an unknotted balloon. If only she had been correct. If only the one with that voice had remained behind. She would like to see his face. Scanning her torn shirt, worn jeans, and tattered, fringed boots, she combed her fingers through the long dark snarls of waist-length hair and shrugged away the discouraged feeling. She would not want to meet a boy looking like she crawled straight out of a dumpster anyway. Still she wondered about his face, his personality, that one kind eye peering through the crack, the deep sapphire shielded by darkness that blocked daylight.

Absently, she stepped away from the barn, her brother yards ahead, whistling like he didn't have a care in the world.

Idiot! He had no fear of anything!

Dry grass crackled beneath her feet as she followed the whistling bird toward the woods. Absently her fingertips continued the grooming of her long dark hair and she let her guard down.

Snap!

The noise followed her; she froze, every muscle

ready to run like a startled deer.

"Stop right there... Don't take another step... Turn around."

It was him— the voice from beyond the wall, the eye peeking through the crack, harshly whispered words like a wild breeze blowing into her ears.

Joyful mischief filled her; a slight smile touched her lips as she turned coyly.

She would see his face.

"What are you doing?" Carmen fisted her hands and pressed them to her hips. The force of her motions swung long, dark corn rows over her left shoulder. Anger deepened her delicate, caramel complexion as she prepared to fight for her belongings. "I said, what are you doing?" Her voice intimidated the thief into glancing over his shoulder.

She was tiny for having such a dominant voice... and beautiful beneath the anger. Too bad she's so young, he thought as he pivoted, empty turned-up palms facing her. "I was looking for something to eat, okay? I haven't eaten in two days. There's nothing out there... nobody's willing to help me."

Her dark eyes squinted and scanned. Was he telling the truth, or was he just another homeless thief looking for valuables to sell for drugs or alcohol? He didn't look homeless. His clothes were too new to the streets. No matter, this bag wasn't her real bag. This bag was a decoy to catch the thief who stole her mother's teardrop pendant— worth more sentimentally than monetarily as they would learn when they went to pawn it.

"Please, I'm really dizzy. I need food, water. Do you know where I can find some?" he pleaded. Carmen almost felt sorry for him, but she'd lived on the streets long enough that her nerves steeled her emotions. Nobody would take her belongings, again. Everything in her bag was all she had left of her parents, her family, her home.

As she eyed the young man before her, his knees buckled beneath him and he crumbled to a heap in the dirty alley.

"Hey! Hey, are you messin' with me? You better not be fakin' it!"

No answer.

No movement.

Carmen tentatively moved toward him. She pushed his shoulder with her worn boot. "Hey, you okay?"

No response.

He must have been telling the truth.

She felt his neck for a pulse, found one.

Lifting his hair, she rested her palm on his forehead. She lightly pinched the skin on his arm and counted to three.

Definitely dehydrated.

Compassion overpowered her own self-preservation code; she would have to share her food before it was too late for him. In spite of the horror in her world, Carmen wanted to believe that everyone still had a good side she could coax out, but dark, muddy green filled the world. Yet, when she first glimpsed this guy, she'd seen gray, splotches of dark gray. Even so, she knew she couldn't trust the colors anymore.

Gripping the young man at his armpits, she began dragging him toward her temporary home. He wasn't light for his size, but she had strength beyond her size. Once inside the mass of pallets, crates, and cardboard, she shrugged loose the bag on her back, unzipped it, and removed a can of chicken broth. It was her last can, one of the many items she'd taken the night she left.

"It's all I got, but it will be the best thing for him." She told herself, propping his head on a mildew scented, worm eaten blanket. Using the church key on her mother's keyring, she punched two holes in the can, one larger, one smaller. She caressed the old house key between thumb and forefinger, forcing the brief thought of loss from her mind.

She lifted his head with one hand and slacked his jaw with the other, then poured a bit of cold, fatty broth into his mouth— not enough to drown him, but enough to stimulate his taste buds, hopefully wake him from his faint. A yellow blob of fat escaped the corner of his mouth, traveled down his chin.

His mouth closed; his tongue and throat worked together to bring the liquid downward. His eyes flickered, opened, stared warily at the cardboard above him.

"Where am I?" His unfocused eyes found her pretty, deep, dark gaze shrouded by long curling lashes, the smooth caramel face of a young girl, the can of chicken broth. "Thank you!" He managed a weak smile, his lids falling closed, again.

"Yeah, just don't get any ideas. You're not stayin'. This is my dive. Took me a long time to put these crates together, find enough plastic to keep the rain out." Her eyes warmly scanned the interior, then coldly returned to his face. She offered more broth. He forced open his eyes and drank it slowly. Elbows bent to push his torso upward as he scooted to lean into the exterior wall of the building serving as one side or her shelter; he took the can from her as he straightened against the brick wall.

"Hey, I can't argue. It's a great place for a pretty, little girl to hide from the masses of bad people out there!" He joked weakly.

"Don't you be gettin' any ideas! And I ain't little. I'm fourteen!" She argued.

"Well, it's nice to meet you, fourteen. I'm," he frowned, confusion filling him, "lost." Leaning into the brick wall behind him, he stuck his right hand out to her. She refused it.

"Just drink your broth— slowly— then get out." She sat back, watching his every move.

"Yes, ma'am!" He saluted. Tipping the can to his lips, he tilted his head back... and fumbled the half empty can when his eyes viewed the makeshift ceiling. The map, or flowchart, or whatever she would name it, reflected a memory, and there was little need to study it.

"Who are you?" He lowered the rescued can to his leg, but his eyes never left the ceiling.

"N-O-Y-B! And stop lookin' at my stuff!" She raised her hands to block his view.

"N-O... oh, your business, yeah, okay— no, you don't understand." Rolling onto his left hip, he dug a finger and thumb into his back pocket to remove a folded, heavily worn paper. After setting the can of broth aside, he pulled the delicate corners apart with care. Holding the paper corners gently, he crossed his forearms flipping the drawing toward her.

"How far away is it, Nathan?" Cai asked as she laid out silverware.

"Back of the property, in an old pasture connected to the neighbor's place. No houses around it. At least, that's the one that's been left boarded up as long as I can remember. We can check it out later," Nathan forked a slice of ham into the pan, the sizzle bringing hunger pangs to the five others gathered in the kitchen. Splash tilted his nose up and sniffed the air, as thankful for Nathan's grandfather's cellar as anyone else in the room.

"Does anyone think it's odd that none of *them* have been back?" Jaz suspected the worst as he perused the pantry shelves. "They just left all this food? All that time they were here?"

"Maybe they poisoned it all!" Rebecca joked and patted Splash's head.

"They probably stocked up for stake outs and meetings. Remember how many cars were here that first time we drove by?" Thad pointed out.

"Considering those cars, there is something weird about this. I mean, Jaz is right, nobody has shown up since those men in the woods disappeared. Why? I don't like it. I don't like staying here. I think we should find somewhere else, or just go out and look for the others. I think this might be a trap. It's too easy, like the first time we were h..." Cheater eyed Jaz and nervously drummed her fingers on the kitchen table.

Nathan cringed at the thought of strangers taking over his home like that. A feeling of invasion crept through him, like somebody was watching him. Though he tried not to think about it, the night he left his grandparents for dead replayed in his mind every second he spent in the house. Being home was not a good idea. Fear slithered through his mind and through his emotions. "Yeah, well, Charles said he would take care of it. Still, staying here is just too ..."

"...dangerous," Jaz interjected, trying to steer Nathan's thoughts back to the mission. They couldn't have Nathan falling apart now. Jaz and Cai discussed earlier how much Nathan had changed the past few days. Truthfully, they were all on edge waiting for the inevitable.

"Yeah, dangerous," Nathan glanced at Jaz and nodded an appreciative smile. Biting his lower lip to stem the tears, he returned his attention to the stove.

Behind his back, Cai sent a concerned look around the table. None dared to think about that look. Nathan's emotions had been all over the place. If they even shared a thought, he would intercept it and go berserk, like yesterday.

"You know, I don't know why there would be any interest in that old hay barn. Grandpa said he boarded it up because too many teens were sneaking into it, leaving beer bottles and trash all over. He got tired of cleaning up their mess while the sheriff never took action."

"There has to be a reason why they wanted this place, why we were all led here. Somewhere on this property is something they want, or maybe something connected to us," Cheater suggested. They'd searched the house, the cellar, the sheds nearest the house. They'd practically torn down the old garage walls.

Nothing.

"Yeah, but maybe they already found whatever it is," Thad interjected. "Maybe that's why nobody's been back."

"Then why the big fight? Why not just walk away and let us have the place?" Nathan's anger rose. It was the only reason Cheater could deduce for not having been able to channel his grandparents. They needed Nathan's anger. Jaz, Cai, Nathan... the three emotionally charged ones. Were there three more like them?

"Maybe to scare us?"

"Rebecca's right. Maybe it was just a control move, like strategizing, you know, like chess," Jaz shrugged.

Five sets of eyes scanned Jaz's tough features. "Chess?" their voices blended as one.

"Okay, a'right! Sheez! Piano, chess... I was like that. Shut up!"

They snickered at the contrast of past and present Jaz, from cultured to tough guy.

"And you were like that because of your mother. We would all have done anything for our mothers." For the first time since they'd banded together, Rebecca silently reached an uncertain hand toward Jaz's forearm and patted lightly, stiffly, bringing a shy smile from the young boy. Blushing, he peered down at his empty plate, understanding the significance of what she had just said, done. For her, proximity, social contact, wasn't easy.

While they ate breakfast, Nathan drew a rough map of the property, placing an X near every building he could remember. "It's a big place, though. This is gonna take a while. Grandpa used to have lots of cows, different hay barns, buildings."

"What about underground buildings?"

"Maybe. I'm not sure. Besides the cellar, yeah... sure... there could be others."

"I'd say, let's eat, clean this up and get started then. It could be a long day searching for something that may not even exist." Cai gathered the empty dishes and placed them in the sink. "Who's day is it?"

No answer.

"Come on. We have to have some order around here. Nathan cooks; the rest clean." She shrugged, hands before her, palms up.

"Ugh! Mine," Thad fessed up. "I hate doing dishes!"

"I know. I'll help you so we can get out of the house quicker," Jaz thumped the younger boy's shoulder.

Half an hour later, the six passed through the back door remaining alert to possible dangers though there had been none since they took back the house. The three dogs lead the way as if reading the human minds, knowing exactly where to stop and sniff.

"Maybe we should split up?" Thad leaned forward, plucked a tall strand of grass as it loomed before him.

"No, we should never split up! We're stronger together. If it takes us two days or more to search this property, we will not split up!" Cai ordered.

Silence followed the motherly tone. The few birds that remained during the mild Texas winter circled above, three of them buzzards spiraling high in the cool morning breeze. Cheater watched their silhouettes against the blue sky, hand shielding her eyes from the bright sun. Unlike most, she didn't find buzzards gruesome. They had a job to do, like the six of them—a mission of sorts. They cleaned up the dead flesh in the world, the garbage collectors of the earth. No, they weren't the most beautiful fowl, but their job was just as important as that of The Gifted Ones.

The dream Cheater had the night before nagged at her as the dark wings circled. She hadn't dreamt of the faceless man, the fire, the cruelty inflicted on the less fortunate of the world. She'd dreamt about... a superhero, of sorts. At least, he seemed to be a superhero. She couldn't figure out why, though. Why— of all things to dream about— dream about the Dark Knight? They hadn't even turned on the TV in the living room since they'd been in the house. They'd been too busy planning, plotting, and learning about each other.

Where had that dream come from? The last superhero movie she'd seen was with Sadie... the newest Spiderman movie. The Batman of her dream was different from the Batman of old, of the movies. He was... new, muscular, or his costume was.

She recalled in her dream that Batman had been hiding. The revelation puzzled her. She didn't understand why. He was a superhero— why hide? And who was he hiding from?

Closing her eyes, she forced the dream to return, replay in her mind. Just as the Batman-like face turned up toward hers— droplets of rain water racing toward his chin— Nathan stopped and she plowed into his back, almost knocking him off his feet.

"Oh, gosh! Nathan, I'm sorry! Are you okay?" Cheater gripped his elbows to steady him.

"What the ...?" He spun off balance, fists clenched at his sides, then relaxed when he saw the fear in Cheater's eyes. Cheater swallowed, sighed, and forced back tears.

"I'm sorry you guys. I'm sorry," Nathan dropped to his knees allowing the grief to fill him. His shoulders shook as he knelt on the dry ground below, hands shielding his face. The Gifted Ones searched each other's eyes, afraid to move, then Cheater knelt beside Nathan boldly wrapping her arms around him and squeezing, "It's okay. It's all going to be okay. We're all together. We'll help you get through this, Nathan." Words of sympathy fell on deaf ears as Nathan released the grief his anger had buried deep inside. He couldn't pen it up any longer. Her numerous losses flowed between reminiscence of his grandparents. The other four dropped chins to chest and stared at the ground while darkness clouded their vision.

"Nathan, look!" A surprised Cheater prodded,

shaking Nathan's tense shoulders.

When Nathan allowed his hands to fall away, he turned eyes upward where his grandparents and parents stood before him.

"It just takes a little grief, a little desperation, a little humility..." Cheater smiled to herself, now understanding the power she'd carried for so many years, the warm darkness that embraced her.

Nathan wiped his cheeks, pushed up from his knees and stood before the others, a calmness filling his features. The old anger was gone, but in its place a new determination the others hadn't seen. He was ready to complete the mission he was born to fulfill— whatever it might be. They'd been worried that his homecoming would change him, and it had. Now, he spurred them onward, a second in command, and before long they'd reached the first old outbuilding during relaxed, lighthearted conversation.

"Yeah, so who's the one that dreams of Batman?" Jaz teased.

"You know you can't keep secrets from us, Cheater," Thad playfully pushed her shoulder with his fingertips.

She shrugged, "Hey, what can I say? At least

he wasn't on fire! And he had a face... a masked face, but still he had a face!" A brief look of concern shadowed her features as she compared the face to the one without.

"Think there was more to the dream than just that?" Cai called from around the corner of the worn wood building.

"I don't know. I can't remember the whole dream, but something important happened. I kind of feel like I know the guy dressed like Batman."

"From a foster home? The Children's Home? Where?" Rebecca prodded.

"No. No, I've never really met him before. I remember faces. But I just feel like I know him, or should know him."

"Ah, so it's like that... future boyfriend?" Nathan raised his brows and nodded at Cheater.

"Dork!" Cheater shook her head.

"You think he's one of us?" Cai tilted her head to peer around the corner at the others.

"Seriously, Cai? That would be ironic. A superhero dressed like a superhero!" Jaz loosed a laugh from the depths of his abdomen and cut it off midway. The five glanced at each other, the same question creasing their brows. "It was just a joke..." Jaz broke the silence. Five questions followed.

"Are we..."

"Is that... "

"Could we..."

"How could..."

"Is it..."

"What if..."

Six unified voices shared the same disbelief, the same answer.

"Nooo!"

Heads shook.

Noses crinkled.

Eyes wondered.

Was it possible?

The pursuing silent tension, the thoughts and questions, broken with Cai's order, "Let's just see if we can find a way into this old building, huh? Can't be too hard. I mean, look at this wood! It's practically falling away from the nails."

Curiously, the six eyed each other as they searched for loose, rotted boards or wide openings.

"Hi, there ..." Neka flipped dark hair over her left shoulder with a toss of her head.

"I said don't move!" The young man halfheartedly pointed the gun from his waist.

"I didn't, hottie..." Neka winked.

"Stop that! Do you know how much trouble you're in?"

"And just how do you define *trouble*?" A glint of reflected sunshine drew his eyes to the top of her head where her near ebony hair parted on the left side. A slight tilt allowed shimmering hair to cover her right eye. He was temporarily entranced by her beauty when he made eye contact.

"Are you alone?"

"Mhm, *so* alone." She pouted.

"I said stop that! With any other person, you'd be in a lot of trouble acting like that." At that moment, his stern look reminded her of her father; shame briefly shadowed her charm.

"Oh. You mean you like g..."

"No, that's not what I meant. I mean, you need to have more respect for yourself, for who you are... what you are... and you need to get out of here before the others arrive."

"Others who? Wait— you're letting me go?" Confusion wrinkled her nose.

"Yes. Meet me at the field house after dark, around 10. I'll explain there."

"Field house? Where— do I know you?" Neka frowned.

"No, but I know you. Now, go!" Gripping the pistol by its butt, he let it rest near his thigh as she followed his command. Neka shot a confused frown over her shoulder before disappearing into the wooded area where Nashota waited.

"Okay... you know I can see you, right?" The tall figure stood over him, huge, muddy sneakers plastered with leaves and wet grass. The size alone scared him into a trance-like stillness. "I'm not gonna hurt you." The shoes and the pitch of the voice didn't add up, and though he still feared the speaker wearing those sneakers, he threw his cape off as he rolled out from beneath the Juniper to stand.

A heavy breath filled his lungs.

"What's your name? And don't tell me it's Batman because he wouldn't be all stuck up under that tree afraid of my shoes!"

He frowned. The voice above him knew of Batman?

His eyes shifted upward, but his neck straightened at the waist before bending backward to peer up. Afraid to look further, he stared at the waist. He exhaled. Whoever this person was could probably pound him with a hammer fist into the soggy ground like a steel post— in one whack.

Batman would not be afraid.

Batman wasn't real, either.

He'd already been overly afraid once, and too slow. He cringed at the memory.

Never again.

Face your fears.

His eyes roamed from mid-trunk upward. Paintbrush ends of blonde braids rested at eye level. This was the tallest girl he'd ever seen, and that included any past college basketball players whose autographs he collected when his dad took him to home games. This girl had to be almost eight foot tall!

A satisfied smile crinkled her downturned face doing nothing to stifle the shock in his eyes. "Wow!" he mouthed.

"Yeah, yeah, I know. I'm the tallest girl you've ever seen. I hear it all the time. No, I never played basketball, and I don't have an interest in it, either. You might want to close your mouth. A fly just flew in there and came back out. Out of toothpaste?"

When he didn't comply, she bent her elbow and gently forced his chin upward with her index finger. His jaw fell slack again when she let go.

"Sheez! You're making me uncomfortable!"

As she thought about smacking his cheek, his jaw snapped shut and he frowned up at her, "You were gonna slap me?"

"How'd you know that?"

Realizing he'd given up his secret to a stranger, he turned away nervously, "I— I felt it."

"Huh, you must have known you needed it. Come on. Let's get out of here before we get caught. There's a house nearby, a big farm. Maybe we can find you something to wear besides that terrific costume. You kind of draw attention, you know?"

"Me?" Eyes wide, he tapped the muscular plastic chest of his costume with his thumb.

A deep laugh filtered down as the girl turned away. He trailed her long stride, two steps to her one, water pooling in the fresh indentations left behind by her gigantic shoes.

"Where did you get that? Who gave it to you? Someone from 'round here?" Carmen reached for the delicate, yellowing paper, but the strange boy pulled it away.

"Nah, you aren't takin' this. I've had this for... well, as I don't actually remember. It belonged to... somebody I knew." Brows furrowed, Simon gently folded the paper.

"They're... they're identical..." Carmen whispered, her eyes turned to the image above her.

"I know. When did you draw that? Why? Have you seen it before?"

"Yes, in the book... I memorized it from a book... the book with my favorite fairytale in it... the one my mom read to me ev—"

"Every night? Wait! Like clockwork? The same time every night... the same story... I'm starting to remember..."

"What's wrong with you? Are you okay?"

"I just... can't remember..."

"Wait? Do you know your name?"

"Simon... I think. At least, that's the name on this paper." He lifted the folded paper by a corner and waved it toward her.

"You don't know? Do you like, have amnesia or something?" Carmen sat back, eyes watching his every move.

"What are you talking about?" Simon's

confusion caused her concern. Her mother had been a nurse before... Carmen learned about concussions and malnutrition. "Have you ever heard of a place called Paradise?"

"It sounds like I should know it, but I just don't —" Simon tilted an ear toward the ceiling as if listening to voices.

"Look, I think you might have a concussion or something? Were you hit in the head recently? Is it okay if I feel around your skull?"

"I don't know, but yeah, sure." He blinked several times. "Paradise?" He whispered, bending his head forward as her fingers gently slipped through his hair.

"I want to say it's in some kind of story? A story that... Ouch!" He yelped as her fingers slid over, stopped, and lightly pressed on an egg sized lump.

"Great! Starved and injured... how did you get the goose egg?" Carmen tilted his chin upward and turned his head toward the sun lit opening of her hovel. She slid her right palm over first one eye then the other, paused after each, and let her hand fall away checking the reaction of each of his pupils.

Simon searched his hands, his lap, "I'm sorry, a... a goose egg?"

"The lump on your head, Jack!" Carmen had no patience. Time was not on her side in the matter of her mother, and this problem took more time from her.

"Oh, I don't know... I don't remember... I..."

Carmen huffed. "It'll come back to you. Finish your broth." She crossed her legs, a frown creasing her brow.

"It's Simon, not Jack. I think." Simon swallowed and watched her puzzle over his comment before chuckling. "I guess we both have stuff to figure out."

"Well, Simon it is, for now. Yeah, we'll figure it out." Carmen shoved a few items in her real bag and rolled out of the box. "But I will tear down that ceiling before we go anywhere. You stay here. You need more food and some ice for that head." She called back.

"No, wait. I'm fine. Let me go, too. I'll find food later." When he moved, dizziness overtook him.

"Ha, not funny. 'Less you got some money you don't remember having." Carmen turned toward him walking backward, palms out.

"Uh, no. I don't have any money. I don't think..." Simon patted his pockets.

"Just wait here. There's a dumpster around the corner— behind a restaurant. Sometimes, they throw away orders that ain't been picked up. Not often, but sometimes. I'll be back." Carmen promised.

"A dumpster? Yuck!"

"When you're homeless and hungry, you don't care where your food comes from." Carmen turned toward him and shrugged.

"How do I know you'll come back? You're taking your bag with you."

"It's my bag and you are nosey. I'll be back. Ain't gonna let you starve to death. I'll help you rest up and get well, then I'll split!" Carmen yelled before disappearing around the corner.

"A dumpster? Really?" Simon shook his head until a sharp pain pierced his skull. His nose wrinkled and he cringed. "Am I that hungry?" Leaning into the cardboard box, his head spun and he balanced in a squat, flat palms and feet on the ground, before resting against the cold, cardboard covered bricks, "I think I'd rather die. Or, did I die? Why do I think I died?" He took in the interior of the scant shack, then turned his attention back to the spiral.

"S'up? Ya' find anything? A way in?" Cai poked Thad in the shoulder after rounding the corner of another dilapidated barn. With all the rotten wood, she thought, there should be an easy way in.

Thad's thumb pressed into the cool teardrop shaped object in his pocket, his head snapped up and he peered into the woods. Should he tell her?

"It amazes me how sometimes your mind can be completely blank like that! How do you do that? Ever since we learned to hear thoughts, I've been able to tap into the others whenever I want, but you... there are times you seem just blank. Nobody's mind is ever blank, Thad.

"Hey, are you listening to me, Thad?" Cai's hand squeezed his shoulder.

Pulling his own hands free, he glanced at her and pointed to the fresh footsteps near his feet, reluctant to share the discovery with her, "Look. They came out here, but there's no door there." He nodded toward the cracked wood of the barn wall.

Cai's eyes followed his finger up. She frowned. "One of us?" she wondered. "Or... one of them?"

"And look out here—" Thad followed the footprints toward the woods, "—one set from the barn, then two here, facing each other."

"Hey, guys! I found some tire tracks over here! Footprints, too!"

Thad glanced at Cai, "Go. I'll follow these tracks."

"No, wait until we get back. The door's probably over there where Jaz found the tracks."

"Okay, but that doesn't tell us how this person came through that wall."

"Just wait here."

Thad did as Cai asked, but only to play the

lame roll he'd always played. His fingers located the object in his pocket and he held it delicately between thumb and forefinger. "Oh, Mom, I miss you so much, but I cannot follow you to my death," he whispered. Besides, he didn't want the others to butt in on his thoughts of the girl in the woods. He knew everything about her, and he knew what he had to do if the opportunity arose.

"Look, tracks all around the barn, but tire tracks here, leaving there. I think it might be in here, whatever they were looking for, and they found it," Excitement flowed brought a tremble to Jaz's words.

"Maybe, but Thad found tracks back there, going toward the woods. It appears that they almost found another one of us, and then did. Funny thing is, the tracks that start toward the woods continue, and the other tracks come back here."

"Maybe the person in the vehicle found the tracks and then left?" Rebecca interjected.

"Without following? Maybe. I'm gonna go back to the other tracks and follow them with Thad. You guys see if you can figure out how to get in this building." Cai peered up toward the roof of the barn searching for windows.

"I'll go with you and Thad," Jaz offered, leading the way around the barn, "just in case."

"Okay," Nathan shrugged, reaching up to pull at a loose board. "We're just gonna have to tear down a door. Sorry, Grandpa!" He called toward the clouds.

"You are so weird," Cheater worked her fingers into the cracks on either side of the board as he forced the hammer claw in, the loose board creaking with each push on the handle, nails popping loose from the worn wood.

"Where are they?" The voice grumbled from behind the chair back, the speaker turned to the window view in the leather executive chair. He took in the cityscape beyond, clouds building to a coming storm. Just the way he liked it.

"Still scattered, boss. We could round them up pretty easily now. They're close." The chair whirled. Hands slapped the desk. Stormy eyes pierced the assistant's abdomen. Fingertips lifted from the edge of the mahogany desk, fading prints slowly dissipating.

"No! I'm just getting impatient. I need them to be together. I need them to find it, open it. That's when they will be at their weakest point, when they're trying to figure it out." He spun the chair toward the window again.

"But, boss, their power grows as they unite, doesn't it?"

A long pause.

A deep inhale.

A frustrated sigh.

"How many times do I have to explain?" His enraged voice reverberated through the nearly empty office space. He threw fists in the air and whirled the chair in rage as he rose, the handsome face twisted in ire; the dark eyes flashed.

"They are nothing without their precious hand-me-downs, and I've already acquired most of them. I can use that to my advantage. Then, I will know every move they make, every thought they think..." he paused.

"Still, they are so slow— stupid children! Patience was never to my credit. I've done everything possible to lead them to this point in time. Their powers belong to me, should have been given to me!"

A long, deep inhale, "They are almost here. I can wait. My hope right now is the boy, the one on the inside. My plan cannot fail. One month from now, their power will be mine; this country, this world, will be mine. No one will be able to stop me." A grin twisted his features and his eyes reddened behind the darkness. His aide winced, turned away to protect himself from the evil power leaking from every pore in his boss's flawless features. "One month. I can wait. Let them gather at that dilapidated, stinking, old farm. As a matter of fact, call off the sheriff's department and any other law enforcement we have leading them. I want them to find *it* without fear of being caught. I want them to get to know each other, let their powers grow and mingle."

"Uhm... you sure that's such a good idea, boss? You don't think they'll suspect something if we suddenly stop looking for them?"

"Ugh! Shut up! Get out! You cannot play devil's advocate with the devil!" The tall man turned his back on the retreating servant. Lightning flashed behind the man, beyond the glass as the dark clouds roiled and pressed their way toward the city. He smiled at visions of destruction he created in his mind, tumbled buildings, fires and flying debris killing many who didn't follow him. If that boy were here now, right now in this moment...

"Yes, patience." He nodded, glancing at the large, locked drawer of his desk.

He sighed.

"When their power is at maximum capacity, when they have lighted the way, I will rip out their strength and cast their weak, simple minded shells to the heavens! This is my world! Those silly women had no right to..." he calmed himself before he let the next words slip.

"This way, Batman."

"I told you, stop calling me that! It's just a comic con costume. *My name is Jamie.*"

"Right. I'd go with Batman... or James. Well, hopefully you are about to get rid of that costume. Look straight through these trees."

Jamie peered through the thicket. An old barn leaned eastward, and around the barn door, two teenagers worked at loosening a board. "Do you know them?"

"Uh, no! But look, he's gotta be about your size. Where there's a guy your size, there's clothes your size, right?"

"Maybe. But don't you think they'll report us to the cops or something?" Jamie frowned.

"No, I don't. I've been here before," Lena paused. "You know how hard it is for someone my size to hide in the woods? Anyway, you should have seen the fight those six kids put up to take this farm.

If I hadn't been strong enough to push out of that cop's trunk, I wouldn't have seen it. I'd have drowned."

"Trunk? Drowned?" Jamie stared at the two kids. "Wait, *you* fit in a trunk?"

"Yeah. It wasn't easy for that cop, either. After I followed those kids here, I watched that guy right there heal a bullet wound in his leg." She slipped the rifle scope from her back pocket. "Never had any use for guns, but this thing comes in handy. Took it off the cop's rifle in the trunk." She bounced it in her hand.

"Where is here, anyway?"

"An old farm in Paradise, Texas."

"Paradise... wait!" He whispered thoughtfully.

"Yeah, does that mean something to you?" Lena glanced over at him.

"Just reminds me of an old story." Jamie frowned, remembering his mother's voice. "Hey..." he paused, realizing he didn't know her name.

"Lena. That's my name," She looked down at his bat ears and frowned. "Yes, it's the same old story my mother told me," Lena nodded.

"My mother used to tell me about twelve kids, a monster... w... are they... are we..." Jamie looked up at her.

Lena nodded. "You're slow. Yes, they are and we are. That's the story! Twelve Gifted Ones! I think so." It was Lena's turn to frown and sigh.

Jamie turned his eyes back to the teens at the barn.

"Yeah, we are. They are. We've arrived exactly where our lives have led us." Sadness the realization filled each word Lena spoke before she jerked her head toward Cheater and Nathan. "I've been a little afraid to walk up on them alone."

Jamie gasped, "You? Afraid? Wow!" Jamie turned his attention back to Cheater and Nathan. "Wow!" he repeated.

"Looks like they're the only ones around. Think maybe they could use a little help with that door?" Lena asked.

"You don't think they'll like, attack us or something?" Jamie stumbled along behind Lena as she crashed through the thicket making more noise than a bull moose in rut.

"Yo, Gifted Ones!" Lena raised a hand. "Need some help?" Cheater and Nathan froze, their backs toward the newcomers. Slowly, they turned, their gazes leaving each other to focus on the two approaching.

"The giant footprints," Nathan whispered in awe.

Darkness pushed back the blue above them as they sprinted toward the house, the heavy drops pinging metal roofs and siding.

Cai pushed the door open as Jaz leaped over the steps to the threshold, "Find anything?"

"No. Nothing." He searched the room. "Where's Cheater?"

"Not back, yet. I hope they make it before the storm gets too bad. Those clouds are pretty ugly." Cai peered up as lightning bolts spread across the horizon. "We didn't find anything, either. I'm beginning to wonder if there really is something here for us to find. I mean, it would help if we knew what we were looking for."

"Yeah, what about you, Thad? Did the footprints lead to anything?" The three had split up to follow tracks through the pasture.

Thad turned from the window, "No. Nothing. Nobody."

"I don't like it. It's just too easy. Nobody comes out here all of a sudden, no law... nobody. Why?" Jaz shook his head and turned toward the door, his concern for Cheater and Nathan apparent as he watched the back yard, especially after Nathan's outburst earlier. He began to wish they'd stuck with Cai's initial instinct of staying together.

"It's not a trap, if that's what you're thinking...

I mean, I don't think so. I think they were searching for something, but they either found it, or didn't find it and have learned what we are learning; this isn't the place," Thad offered.

His oppositional comment surprised Cai, her corrective instincts taking over, "They killed for it, Thad. Nathan's grandparents. Whatever it is was is valuable enough for them to commit murder. There has to be something here."

"Hmph!" Thad shrugged and turned away. He pulled out a dining room chair and sat.

"Unh! What does that mean? Since when do you grunt at me? I don't know what's going on with you, Thad, but you've changed since we arrived here. Are you mad about something?"

Thad glanced into her eyes then over her shoulder unable to hide his thoughts from her probing eyes, though he had no trouble hiding them from her mind. She was like a sister to him. He'd never had the kind of affection, attention, protection that she offered him. "I just— I think it's a waste of time looking for something that may not exist, that's all."

"What else are we gonna do, dude? Go to school?" Jaz shook his head. "There's gotta be some clues here somewhere, something that leads us to why all this is happening. The story can't just end like this— at least not the story I know. Because, you know, we still have that whole dream business."

"Right. We just need to keep looking, and the other six should be arriving soon. If nothing else, we should at least wait until we're all together before we leave here." Cai suggested.

"No!" Thad rose from the chair he'd been rocking on the back legs and stomped to the living room window. "Staying here is creeping me out! Those footprints... we should follow their example and get out of here. We should go back to town, check the field house, look around there! I mean, they're like us; that's where we hid."

Frowns of concern passed between Cai and Jaz. "I'm not goin' anywhere till Cheater and Nathan return!" Jaz shook his head at Thad.

"*Me, neither,*" Rebecca stepped cautiously down the stairs, her notebook pages bouncing with each step.

Thad calmed as she entered and was first to greet her at the bottom of the stairs. "Hey!" He smiled. Rebecca cast a doubtful smile his way and continued to the others.

"Matter of fact, I'm gettin' ready to go lookin' for them. I don't like this. *At all!*" Jaz moved toward the back door, but froze in his reach for the door when he glimpsed the figure that pulled back the screen to enter. Lena ducked under the door frame into the kitchen behind Cheater who grinned at the shocked expressions watching their entrance. "Hey, guys! This is Lena."

Lena's golden crown almost touched the kitchen ceiling. Her playful smile eased their fears, "Yeah, nice to meet you, too!" She swung an open palm in a half moon, "and this..." Lena waved the same large hand toward Nathan and Jamie as they entered, "is—"

"Batman!" The other six finished. Lena's laughter reverberated off the walls. With the back of her hand, she wiped away seeping tears from the corners of her eyes. Jamie, hands on hips, waited for a pause in the ruckus, but they laughed harder at his "crime fighter" pose accentuating the costume.

"Very funny!" Jamie rolled his eyes upward at Lena, then scanned the rest of the group. "Jamie!" He yelled over the roar. "Are there any clothes in this place that might fit me?"

"Sure," Nathan shook away a chortle and waved him over. "There may be something upstairs. You're a little taller than I am, but I'm sure we'll find something."

"Speaking of tall..." Cai, a little less than half the height of Lena, tilted her head back to peer up into Lena's downturned face.

"Ran in the family," Lena's grin rounded her cheeks.

"Huh," Cai nodded, "mine, too!"

"Welcome to Hero Headquarters." Rebecca joked.

Lena glanced toward Rebecca, then at the others. "Who said that?"

"You'll get used to it. Heck, soon you'll do it." Thad shrugged to identify himself.

"Whoa!" Lena's lips formed an O. "And all I got is this spectacular figure?" Her hands gestured down her sides as if she were asking for an opinion on a new outfit. "Think you guys will grow?"

The downstairs filled with hoots of hysterics.

Simon tossed and turned. The dream nagged at him. The hard ground grew colder beneath the layered newspapers.

She was back, the dream girl with the wisps of brown hair spidering across her face, the flames licking at her from behind.

"No... no... no!" Simon rolled to his left side where a whiff of hamburger and fries caused his eyelids to blink the girl's image away as his stomach responded to the smell. He glanced at the bag, then at Carmen.

"Are you sure this is safe to eat?" Simon gripped the bag and opened it warily.

"The guy never even opened the bag. He's the first person to have pity on me since I hit the streets. Most people just flinch and ignore me. Wonder why?"

"Uh, maybe your clothes?" Simon frowned at the holes in her shirt and jeans.

"I meant, I wonder why he took pity on me... all

the sudden. Weird." Carmen grew pensive.

Nobody had offered to help her since she left home. Why now? A strange thickness filled the air around her as her suspicions multiplied. Feelings of betrayal battled with curiosity as she opened the bag. She'd watched the bag switch hands from hostess to patron. The patron's color was trustworthy, wasn't it?

"What were you dreaming about when I came in?" Carmen pulled a burger from the bag.

Simon greedily pulled back the wrapper and answered around his chewing as he kept the contents in his mouth from showing, "Girl... fire... I dunno," he mumbled around food.

"Slow down. You'll get stomach cramps. A girl and fire? Long brown hair? Sad face? That girl?" Carmen tilted her head as she handed him a carton of French fries.

"Yeah, her. Who is she?" He shoved a few fries into his mouth.

"You're gonna throw up," Carmen shook her head at him before slipping into thought while she nibbled a fry of her own. Her brows drew downward in contemplation and doubt. "I don't know, but when we finish here, I get the feeling we need to get outta here. Something weird is happening. I can almost touch the change in the air."

"What makes you say that?" Simon savored another bite of burger.

"There's a heaviness in the air. A suffocating heaviness. The streets are turning black. Can't you see it? Feel it?" Carmen fell silent, black shadows creeping into her hovel, reaching toward her, waving tentacles of darkness near her face.

"Like rain? Humidity? Clouds? No. I don't feel it."

"You know what? Let's make this food to-go. I think we better pack up, like right now!" Carmen's panic sent Simon into a state of high alert. He didn't know why he felt the fear broiling from deep within, but somehow it must connect to what had happened to him. If he could only remember what happened.

Stuffing food in his face while helping Carmen remove the hand drawn pieces from the ceiling, Simon asked, "Are we in danger?"

"No, I don't think so... least not yet. That's just it, we are, but we aren't. I know that doesn't make sense, but it's like I'm used to living my life in danger. Now, the air has changed. I mean, cops have been chasing me, people have been turnin' me in, but now, that dude being nice... the dark gray blackness I see everywhere, something ain't right. It *feels* wrong. We gotta go away, far away... fast! Hide out until this grayness blows over."

"Away?"

"Yeah, outta sight... underground... deep. Like the air before a tornado, this thickness is telling me to take cover. That's all I need out of this dive. Let's go!"

Carmen didn't bother exiting the crate and cardboard entry with care. She stood up, bursting through it, essentially tearing down the entire front wall she had so carefully constructed over the past weeks. She worked hard to find all the materials. She didn't want to leave it up for someone else who didn't deserve her kindness!

The sudden light through the opening burst onto Simon's features, making him hurry behind her as fast as his weak state would allow. "I guess the tornado just landed," he mumbled, glancing at the destruction over his shoulder.

Carmen broke into a run as the sun shown above and dark clouds churned, redirecting the light as if leading her way. She wasn't concerned about the weather, the clouds, the thunder roaring in the background. She was, however, concerned about the looks people gave her— about their colors as she passed— and about Simon as he stumbled up the street behind her. It wasn't the type of look she was used to seeing from others. Most ignored her in the streets, unless one was desperate for money and turned her in. The hopeful looks, the frightened looks, the menacing looks to her right and left disarmed her. They weren't the looks of hunger and despair she'd grown used to seeing. They weren't the

I'm-gonna-get-you-where-are-the-cops look she had been fighting all this time.

She was seeing eyes of compassion and concern for her safety, colors of blue and dashes of green breaking through the gray. One homeless guy she'd been fighting with for weeks actually clapped and cheered them on as they passed his makeshift home.

This wasn't right.

None of it was right.

The world was suddenly topsy-turvy.

First Simon shows up, knowing nothing about anything... now this.

Carmen stopped running at a crosswalk to wait for the light to change. Hands on her knees, she doubled forward, inhaled deeply, exhaled forcibly, to catch her breath; she pointed back from where they had come, "Did you see that, those people?"

"Yeah, homeless people? What about them? I mean, why was that dude clapping? Why are we running?" Simon shrugged barely catching up to her to lean against the pole and catch his own breath before the light changed.

A car eased to the curb where they waited. The voice mockingly implied help, "You two need a lift somewhere in Paradise? Someplace like, oh, say Old Towne Road?" The silent red and blue bubbles on top of the car turned Carmen rigid. "I'm sorry Officer, what did you say?" She pretended to care.

Grabbing Simon's hand, she pulled him forward. Beyond the front of the police car, the sound of the officer's hearty laughter faded as he drove away.

"What the heck?" She gasped as she steered Simon through the city under the cover of brush.

Simon pressed fingers and thumb into his right side as he doubled over. Carmen stopped running and tossed her bag off her shoulder to the ground between them. Neither spoke as they rested beneath brush to regain control of their breathing, the sound of thunder closing in above them.

Both searched the wooded area for cover, finding none.

Simon stood, straightened his body— his breathing less desperate— and nodded. As if they could outrun the oncoming storm, the two moved quickly through the wooded area, seeking a path around the small brush and fallen logs along the way. As the rain began, small droplets seeking ground beneath giant oak trees, Carmen and Simon approached a small abandoned building, windows broken, but roof intact. The door squeaked as they moved into the gloomy, cob-webbed, dim interior to wait out the storm.

"Do you think he was serious, about the ride? I mean... what is Olde Towne Road? What's there?"

Simon seated himself in a corner opposite the window on the north side of the small shed. Though the building held warmth from the daytime sun, the cold north breeze fought the warmth for rights through the broken windows from now and again, and Simon shivered in response.

"Yeah, that's the problem. What is there, exactly? Is that where the jail is? I am on the wanted list... a person of interest. Why did he say Paradise like that? Why did he laugh instead of arresting me? He didn't come after us! Something is definitely wrong." Carmen responded in a rush as the ghostly charcoal wisps felt their way through the window and wall cracks of the shed.

Carmen felt the northern through her hair while her head rested against the worn metal wall. She'd closed her eyes against the gray tentacles for protection, but soon she was in the dream, again.

"Morning, Mom! Do I smell waffles? Bacon?" Carmen tilted her nose up and took in the aroma.

"Yes, you do, my love! And as soon as your father gets back from his run..." Carmen's mother slapped the back of Carmen's hand as she reached for a slice of bacon, *"We'll eat breakfast. Do you have any*

pressing matters after school today?" The waffle maker opened and her mom forked two waffles onto a plate.

"No, I don't think so." Carmen reached for the plate and took it to the already set table. She went to the refrigerator to retrieve the milk and orange juice, filling each cup. Then she turned her mom and dad's coffee cups over and filled them.

"I need your help after school so come right home then, okay?" Her mom surveyed the table, "Perfect. Thank you," she planted a kiss on Carmen's forehead as the door opened.

Mom's in a really good mood, Carmen thought, raising her brows at her dad as he frowned curiously at her. Carmen shrugged.

"I'm gonna rinse off real quick. I'll be back in a few minutes," Carmen shrugged knowingly at him as he slipped from the room. Mom has been difficult lately, Carmen thought glancing toward the kitchen. Carmen had heard her parents arguing late at night while she studied.

Of course, it was all about Carmen. Mom was pushing Carmen to study the colors, get in touch with her intuition, and she'd been more desperate about Carmen's learning lately. She'd also reminisced with her daughter about the fairytale. Over and over, every night while they gathered in the family room to watch a movie, Mom had made reference to the fairytale.

Dad rolled his eyes more than once a night. Mom's "VooDoo hogwash" references, as he referred to them, were coming more frequently.

Carmen silently ate her breakfast, glancing back and forth between her parents. She loved them both so much. She only wished they could get along better. Mom couldn't help the way she was raised; neither could Dad. It was a constant struggle for Carmen to watch them drift further apart.

After taking her plate to the kitchen, Carmen kissed her mom on the cheek and looked into her hazel green eyes, vowing to be home right after school to help Mom with whatever task she needed help with. Carmen's dad slid his arm around Carmen's shoulder and kissed her temple. "I hope it's not some hoodoo hogwash!" He whispered, closing the door behind Carmen. She stood outside the door listening as the arguing began again, her mom making her usual threats about leaving with Carmen, returning to the country farm where she grew up. Carmen sighed heavily and fled down the stairs. Out the door and beyond in the streets, she pushed on toward school, her safe zone... until that day.

Carmen was late that evening because there was a lockdown at school. Some kid brought a gun and the principal was alerted to a possible second gun.

When Carmen arrived home, her mother was

gone, the apartment was a wreck, and her dad could not be reached.

In sleep, Carmen rolled her head to her other shoulder, and her eyes fluttered open as the scream pierced her eardrum.

"How much longer?" The heel of a sneakered foot bounced impatiently on the concrete.

"Stop bouncing. You're driving me crazy! Ugh!" Neka peered into the darkness. He had said ten, hadn't he?

Neka replayed the conversation in her mind, but she kept getting stuck on his eyes, those gorgeous blue eyes.

She'd sensed urgency, danger emanating from them, and something more, something Neka very much needed. She'd sensed protection.

Then again, maybe it was just that stupid uniform!

He'd scolded her. Remembering his tone angered her, yet at the same time it comforted her.

Who did he think he was anyway?

Her dad used to get so frustrated with her flirty antics. How many times had he *scolded* her? How many times had he asked her to stop behaving in ways unbecoming a lady. How could she, though? How could she behave decently with a twin brother as wild as Nashota? How could she behave like a lady when she had lost her mother during her formative lady years? How could she not climb trees? Why in heaven would she want to learn cooking and cleaning and medicinal remedies when she could have fun, use her beauty to her advantage?

"Why Papa?" she exhaled, barely a whisper. "Why did you leave us?" She asked the darkness in a normal voice.

"I had to do my job!" A harsh voice answered from the darkness. Neka frowned. Had she imagined it? "Look. You need to lay low. Stop making scenes. They're coming for you, you know? They're coming for all of us, waiting until we're all together."

Neka frowned toward the voice, then toward her brother's still knee. Ensuing silence sent a shock of fright through her body, suddenly making her feel very alone. But she knew he was there, in the shadows, protecting her. "Who are you?"

"Never mind. Hold out your left hand." She followed his command and he palmed a folded piece of paper into it. "There's a farm, just outside of town. We'll go there when I come back. Some of us are already waiting there. Some of us are still on their way. You'll get help there. You'll be safe. And for God's sake, don't act like a common street girl. You're so much more than you realize."

Neka's eyes filled with rage at his insult. "How dare you! Why should I trust someone who has no guts to face me in the light? Who calls me names! You... you..." She lashed out in revenge.

"Lose the temper and stay here. I need to remain on the inside, so I keep up with his plans, but I will take you to that farm after I drop off my partner. I'll get information to all of you somehow. When I drop you off, tell them it's there, the—"

Neka waited.

Silence.

"W—" The crunch of tires on gravel stopped her retort.

"Go that way! Did you call her in?" Heavy steps on concrete.

"Uh, yeah. I was just about to pursue her. She took off that way."

"Were you talking to somebody?" The gruff voice filled with contempt.

"Yeah, this stupid phone! I got a text on my cell about a girl messin' around under the bleachers. I wanted to sneak up on her, but she dodged me when you turned onto the gravel. She headed down toward the store."

"Well, forget pursuit. Get back in the car. We got orders to let her go, anyway. I'll drop you off. I just hoped to bring one of them kids in, but he ordered us to leave it."

"Oh. Okay. Here I thought I was doing good."
The younger officer shrugged.

"Eh, you can't help it; orders changed. Let's get
a good night's sleep. All we can do now is wait." The
older man turned back toward the car.

"Yeah, okay."

Car doors closed.

Tires on gravel.

Neka waited until she was sure they were gone.
Nashota resumed bouncing his foot, "Okay, what do
you think?" He whispered anxiously. Neka held an
index finger to her lips. They had fooled her once
today.

Would that guy fool her again?

Were they just trying to catch her?

She opened her hand and the paper
unwrinkled in her palm.

Was it a trap? The tip of her moist tongue
touched her dry upper lip, then her bottom lip as she
debated.

Leave?

Stay?

*He'd called me a common street girl! The
nerve...*

She searched the shadows below the bleachers
for an area in deep darkness. Squeezing her left hand
closed around the paper, she was just about to ball it

up and toss it when a small object slipped from the folds and landed on her foot. She brushed the top of her foot with her fingertips, located the object, and blindly rolled it between thumb and finger.

Placing the object in her pocket, she unfolded the paper and held it facing a nearby streetlight, but it was no use. She couldn't make out the writing. She pocketed the paper just as Nashota stood and disappeared beneath the shadow of the bleachers. He was headed for the other end, going the long way around the field. Maybe that would be safest, Neka thought, following his lead. Sometimes he wasn't as dumb as he acted.

Neka shivered, rubbing her bare arms to create friction. "You know, any guy but you would give me that jacket you have on!" She scowled at her whistling brother huddled beside her under the shadowing bleachers opposite their previous location.

"I don't think he's coming back..." The whistling paused and returned.

"Why would he tell me he was if he wasn't, *stupid*?" Neka emphasized the last word.

"You're not supposed to say that!" Nashota scolded.

"I can say it if I want. Stop pestering me. Just be ready with your... whatever it is you do." Neka turned away.

Silent nod.

Nashota had always protected her. For as long as she could remember, he'd been by her side, pulling her out of trouble. Through all that had happened to them, he'd been there, with his ancestral power, getting her out of dangerous situations. Neka reminisced, casting a warm glance his way as the whistling stopped; a loving smile touched her lips, and he picked up the whistle, again.

"Ugh!" Neka rose from her spot and turned into the chest of the young officer. His arms circled her waist briefly as she bounced backwards and his hands steadied her wobble. Looking into his shadowed face, his glistening blue eyes, her back straightened, and she moved into the embrace she imagined.

Forcefully, he gripped her shoulders and pushed her to arm's length, "John," he introduced himself sternly.

"Me, Neka," she playfully replied.

"Don't be an idiot! Where's your brother?"

"Right—" Neka glanced over her shoulder, "Ugh! I hate when he does that!

Dawning darkened her features, "Wait! How'd

you know about my brother? He slipped off when we met earlier..."

John's features softened, "I told you. I know who you are. I know you have a twin brother. I know you're a Gifted One." He gripped her elbow and guided her into the darkest area beneath the bleachers.

"A what? I'm not gifted in anything, well, unless you count beauty. I'm certainly not a genius, or have magical powers like some books say my ancestors had, but for looks? Got those! I'm just... I don't know, me."

"You know the story? The one about the twelve teens? The princes and princesses? The kingdom?"

Her eyes rose to meet his sincere gaze. "The story of Paradise? Yes. How'd you... where'd you... I don't..."

"I'm one of them, too. We're like family, the Gifted Ones. The only family we have now. We need to get you and your brother to the farm, to safety, where the rest are staying." John gripped her elbow.

"My family is..." Neka's voice quieted, "...Nashota."

"Come on, it's quite a way to the farm, especially in the dark. We'll have to be careful that we're not spotted by police." John tugged at her elbow.

"But you're a cop! And earlier you said

somebody wanted us all together. Why should I go with you?"

"Yeah, I am a cop, sort of. I'm working on the inside, that's what we needed, what the faction needed. I'm not doing it by choice, though. It was the only way to save my life... and my sister's. I let him think he turned me to his beliefs. I can't be seen with you or any of the others. He doesn't know I'm one of you. At least, I don't think so."

"Where's your brother? We have to get out of here." He started around the back of the bleachers, his hand guiding her when she stopped suddenly and jerked away.

"Why should I trust you? It doesn't make sense to me. None of this does."

The cell phone in his pocket vibrated. "Damn!" He ripped it from the opening, careful to shield the lit screen. "Huh, something's up."

She moved toward the light like a mammoth moth, "What is it?"

The cold rain came quickly again, thundering straight down into the bleachers above and gushing down around them. He pocketed the cell phone before it was drenched and pulled two packages from his back pocket. "They just officially called off the statewide search. There's only one reason he would *do* that." John yelled over the rumbling above him. "Disposable rain slicker," he said, handing her a pouch. "I have one for your brother, too. Where'd he go?"

"Don't worry about him. He'll turn up. He always does." She pulled the slicker over her head. "What search? Who texted you?"

"My boss. The one who was with me earlier, at the barn. The man who took our families, stole our lives, led us here with his demented plan, he's the one calling off the search for you, for us. First he orders us to let you go if we find you, now he's completely calling off the search for the Gifted Ones. That might mean he's found... or..."

"Maybe he's had a change of heart. I mean we all change our minds, right? Maybe something's... "

John stared through the rain at the distorted security light, "No! He would die first. Come on! We have to hurry!"

A block away, John located an unlocked car and slid into the driver's side. "Get in!" He motioned as he pushed the passenger door open.

"Is this your car?" She winced at the torn interior, then at him as he bent forward feeling under the floor mat.

"Ah, perfect. It's nice to count on friends never changing their habits. No, I don't have a car. It belongs to a friend. I wish your brother would turn up. I don't want to leave him behind." John raised up and glanced into the rearview mirror as he turned the key and revved the car.

The silhouette of a head stared back at him through the mirror nodding toward his glance.

"O**K**, maybe I am paranoid. Good reason!" Carmen shrugged the strap free from one shoulder and slung it over the other. "I don't want nobody touchin' my stuff, okay?"

"Sheez. Save a guy's life and you still don't trust him," Simon grinned. "Carry it yourself." He attempted to speed up.

"Been carryin' it myself since I took out, Jack! How's your head? I didn't mean to roll my head onto your bump earlier. I fell asleep."

"Simon, not Jack. My head's fine. Yeah, you were moaning and whimpering the entire time you were asleep. Sounded like a little lost puppy. You okay?" he questioned, studying her silent profile. She was kind of cute for a kid. He was having fun at her expense. In all honesty, he would probably be laying back in that alley dying if not for her. Of course, he would have never been in that alley if it hadn't been for...

What exactly? He couldn't remember how he got to the alley. He felt like he'd been running from something, away from something... someone... running away with a bump on his head.

Now he needed to remember how or why. How did that cop know where Carmen was going? Did they know about the drawing in her cardboard shelter? In his pocket? What exactly was going on?

A stupid fairytale couldn't have brought them together, that's for sure. He'd never believed in that crap, even though his mother kept telling him it was true. Was there more to that old story than his mother let on?

"Yeah, I'm good. It was just a memory— the day I left. You okay?" Carmen slowed when his quickened pace brought a stumble. "Need some water or somethin'?" Simon stopped and held his hands out to counter a sudden burst of dizziness. "Yeah... I mean no. I'm fine." He was trying to be strong, but he had gone three days without water before meeting Carmen.

"Well, probably should drink a little water." Carmen stopped, removed a bottle of water from her backpack and handed it to him as he sat down. She studied him while he sipped.

"Don't you be passin' out on me, again! I ain't totin' your behind all the way to wherever."

He glanced at the football field to his right,

catching a water drop on his chin with the back of his hand. How long had they been walking? How long had it been since they left that shack in the city with the cop? Light from the setting sun— barely visible over the horizon— turned the Western sky deep reddish purple. *Maybe we better find a place to hang out until later,* he thought.

Maybe I can go a little farther.

"Hey, there's some woods over that way. We can hideout over there for a while so you can rest up, and we don't have to worry about being seen." Carmen steadied him by his elbow as he stumbled forward, nodding in agreement.

Carmen glanced at him, concern filling her as he rested. What was his story? She wasn't willing to tell him about her mother's disappearance, so she wasn't about to prod him into remembering his own story. Could she really trust this guy? What if— when he did remember— he learns he was actually sent to capture her? What if he was actually one of the kidnappers that took her mother? Maybe that's how he got the lump on his head. But then, how did he know about the story? And if he couldn't remember what happened to him, how could he remember the story?

She'd dreamed of others who knew about the story, a gathering in Paradise. One of her school friends had heard the story, too, but she dismissed it

71

as just another fairytale. Carmen remembered when her teacher read fairytales to them in class— oh, how Carmen loved hearing them— she compared each tale to her own; but how her friend would cringe, hating every magical word of the "fairy nonsense" the teacher read.

Why did the story link her and Simon— and moreover, why did he have the same drawing? Why was the brown haired girl in her nightmare, too? Not only that girl, but the others in the dream as well. Who are they? Were they the Gifted Ones, as the brown haired girl had called them? Simon finished the water in the bottle as she contemplated the answers. He lay back in the damp leaves and grass, crossed his arms over his chest, and took deliberate, deep, calming breaths.

"You need more water. I'm gonna go get ya' some. Stay here."

"No! No, don't leave me here, please!" He tried to push himself up from the ground, but he was too weak.

"Stay here! I'll be back. I promise."

The world spun as Simon raised his head. He laid back in the damp grass. "Fine, I'll stay here." He knew from anatomy class that a body would give out without proper nutrition and water. Weakness would set in and sleep would overtake the body. Simon closed his eyes, trying not to think about the hamburger and fries he'd eaten earlier as his stomach growled again. He felt his body giving in to the sweet temptation of nothingness. He'd longed to feel nothingness since his world changed forever. He opened his eyes, searching the sky above him. *What changed?* He thought. *Where did that come from?* Searching his memory for more information, he shut his eyes, relaxing into the darkness.

Simon assumed the darkness of death was taking over, swallowing him up, luring him to nothingness, but nothingness became a dream.

Simon stood smiling, facing a drummer, his fingers dancing over the bass guitar, head bobbing to the music. His best friends in the world were near, rehearsing the song they'd written together, the garage filled with the tune. A woman opened the garage door and announced dinner to the band.

Her face was familiar to Simon. In the dream he smiled at her, nodded. When the song ended, she clapped. "Encore!" She grinned at the group.

"Be back in a minute, Mom!" Simon ran out to a car parked across the street. Pulling open the passenger door, he reached in for a bouquet of flowers, a gift for his mother on her special day. He'd

saved for a month to buy her the dozen roses in the vase he now gripped in his hand. Through the driver side window he looked up as his world crumbled— the moment he lost his mom and his friends.

Shards of shingles and splinters of wood showered down on him, on the top of his car, in the yards next to and across the street.

"Noooooo!" He rose, his scream filling the starlit sky. Then... then... he woke up in the alley with a lump on his head.

"Is he dead?" Through his dream state, Simon felt a poke in his side.

"Stevie, that's a horrible thing to say and do! Stop poking him this instant!"

"But Ma, he looks dead. Think somebody killed him and left him here?" Poke. Poke.

"I didn't kill him, but I left him here! Now get away from him!" Carmen pushed Stevie aside and peered into Simon's face.

Slap! Slap! Slap!

"Wake up, dang it! You can't give up now! We're too close!" Carmen yelled inches from Simon's nose.

"Can we help? We're actually looking for some friends that might be able to help you. I'm pretty sure they can, but if not, I will be happy to help you." The woman knelt next to Simon and gripped Carmen's wrist as the young girl raised it to slap Simon a fourth time.

"Thank you." Simon smiled weakly, squinting into the face of the woman.

"Oh!" Relieved, Carmen sat back on her heels, "Thank God! I thought you were dead!"

"Not yet. However, if you want to torture me some more..." The woman glanced at him, then at Carmen.

"He's jokin', Ma'am. I only just met him this morning."

"You wouldn't by any chance know about a fairytale, a fiery dream and Paradise?" The woman asked them.

Simon and Carmen glanced at each other then back at her.

"Yup. I told you Momma! They are two of 'em. We need to get a message to those others, a message from Maive. Are you goin' to see them?"

"Stevie! You don't know these people! You don't know if they are..."

"Oh, yes! They are Momma. No other kids their age would be wonderin' around in areas like this. Or be in such poor shape. They'd be with friends or at home or someplace else with friends or maybe at school, I guess. Teenagers don't hang out in the

woods these days! I know, because that's where I
hang out."

The mother smiled and gently touched her
boy's cool cheek.

"So you know about the fairytale, the others?
There really are others?" Carmen's hopeful gaze
turned to Stevie.

"Oh, yes ma'am and they changed our lives
forever, just like they're gonna change yours... well,
when we find 'em, any ways. They're here in Paradise
somewhere."

"We're in Paradise?" A sigh and smile of peace
spread over Simon's face. His eyes fell closed, again.
"I did die," he joked weakly.

"Yes, you are and no you don't. He ain't gon'
make it to see them others if you don't give him more
water. I'll get some," Stevie left the wooded area,
opened the car door, and reached for a bag. He
returned with two more bottles of water.

"As soon as he feels up to it, let's get him to the
car. We'll find the others together. I have some
directions, but they aren't very clear." The woman
fluttered over Simon, checked his forehead with her
palm, his heart rate with her fingers. "He's just
restin'."

"I'll get 'im up!" Carmen slid her arms beneath
his shoulders.

"I can help!" Stevie moved to Simon's other

side.

"No..." Simon moaned in protest.

"Drink some water and shut up!" Carmen ordered.

"Oooh, *Momma*, she said somethin' bad!" Stevie's eyes rounded waiting for the correction his mother normally provided. His mother looked at Carmen, and both stifled their giggles behind thinly veiled smiles.

"That's better!" Jamie skipped the bottom two stairs to turn a circle before the others, holding his arms out as darkness reached through the blinds brightening the indoor lighting. "No ears. No cape. No mask. Now I won't stand out as much."

"Aw, no more Batman? Oh, well. At least I got to hang out with the Black Knight for a little while," Lena joked.

"Yeah, that *was* kind of comforting, seeing Batman. I felt like he might be coming to the rescue," Cheater grinned. "Though, I'm more a Spiderman fan."

"I ain't seen you climb nothin'," Jaz teased. Cheater wrinkled her nose at him.

"Is there anything to eat around here? I'm starving!" Jamie glanced toward the kitchen.

"Me, too!" Lena nodded. "I could use a bite, or ten." The others turned toward her with the same concerned expression. "Don't worry, I don't eat as much as you think I would. I'm just a normal girl."

"Lena, there's not a normal girl in this room!" Cai rose from the chair to help them.

Light reflections flickered through the slits in the living room drapes gliding across the wall opposite Jaz. He jumped to his feet, "Car!" With back to the wall next to the window, he peeked out the window from the side of the drapes. He was right. He knew they hadn't given up on them. Jaz suspected this to be a trap, and sure enough, it was.

"Blend!" Cai ordered.

"What?" Jamie's confusion prompted Cai to grab his left hand. "Lena, take his right and join hands with Nathan. Jamie stumbled as Lena tugged him toward the others. With the line complete, he felt his body changing, molecules moving, shimmering, separating—panic overtook him when he looked at what used to be his feet. "What the...?"

Nothing but hardwood flooring.

He searched the room for the others finding only walls, chairs, bookshelves, lamps, a staircase. The mirror directly across from where he stood showed only the kitchen behind him. Where was he?

Knock, knock, knock.

Silence.

The doorknob at the front turned and the door creaked open. A pretty dark haired girl with glistening brown eyes searched the room right to left, "Nobody's here. Well, I say that, but I feel like somebody's watching me. You know? That uncomfortable feeling you get in the shower sometimes?" Carmen could see colors, a rainbow of shadows in the living room, like people were there, but they weren't. Carmen frowned curiously as she scanned the bright colors in the room; for the first time since the day she left, she felt safe.

Jamie's chest wanted to burst out the breath he'd been holding. How much longer did he have to wait? He couldn't hold his breath that long. Who were these people, anyway? The girl was kind of cute.

"Ah, they're here!" A young boy's head peeked in around the door frame.

"Stevie!" The blend released as Jaz let go, happy to see the young boy again.

"Told ya'!" Stevie ran to squeeze Jaz's waist. "I sure missed you!" Stevie's voice cracked with emotion.

"Stevie, mind your manners! We have a message from Maive for you all. She ain't doin' well. She wanted us to hand deliver it." Stevie's mother entered the room, "And on the way, we found these two. Stevie swears they belong to you."

"They do, Jaz! Momma, they do! Don't ya' Carmen?" Carmen couldn't help but grin at the young boy wrapped around the older one. They were like brothers, really close brothers. Carmen forced back the burn of tears. She was too tough to show tears, but Cheater noticed her hard swallow.

"Hey, Carmen! I'm Cheater, uhm, Sarah. Who's that guy you're holdin' up?"

"Is he okay? What's wrong with him?" Nathan moved to Simon's side to relieve Carmen.

"Eh, he's just not tough like me," Carmen chuckled. "This is Simon. He stumbled into my humble abode this morning about half dead. Nothing really wrong with him. A little hungry. A little thirsty. Well, maybe a lot of both. How'd you guys disappear and reappear like that?" Carmen jerked her chin toward them and stiffened her spine.

Cheater laughed and grabbed her hand. "We didn't really disappear. Come on."

What better way to test her than to teach her? They joined hands again pulling Carmen along. "Watch! This is cool!" Stevie nodded to Simon who was more alert than he had been when Stevie poked him in the side.

"Wait! Carmen, ask about the..." Simon's

voice trailed to silence as Carmen's body blended into the background. "Where is she? What did you do with her?" Simon stumbled toward Carmen, mustering what little strength he had left and almost nose dived into the carpet, but Carmen broke the blend and caught him mid fall.

"We don't have time to show and tell!" Carmen's urgent words forced the teens to action. "It's okay, Simon. Come on, let's get you some water, food. You are too weak!"

Lena moved to Simon's side, "I got him. You go on to the kitchen to see what you can find that will be easy on his stomach!" Lena cradled the passed out Simon like a baby and carried him to the couch. Cheater smiled at the others, then she nodded to Stevie's mom, "Yes ma'am, they belong to us, and we'll take it from here!"

Cheater scanned the nine others, the lost feeling of family returning to her heart. This time there was no fear of losing them, because she knew if one was lost, they would all be lost. They would be together for the rest of their lives, whether that was a day, a month, a year, or many years from now, they would be together.

A tear escaped down her cheek as she watched giant Lena mother the newcomer Simon. She wiped the droplet away as she heard Carmen's strong voice call from the pantry,

"There's enough food in here to feed the homeless on Glory Lane!"

Nathan answered, "You should see the cellar."

The bustle of noise from the kitchen overwhelmed Cheater's senses. She'd spent so much time alone, even with the various families and homes, she had still been alone. Most of her new family had been alone, too. Now here they were, getting close to the time when the twelve would be together. What was to become of them?

"Hey, you okay, Sis?" Jaz picked up on her absence and found her, placing a brotherly arm around her shoulder, placing a light kiss on her temple.

"What's going to happen to us, Jaz?" She looked up into his concerned eyes.

"Whatever is meant to happen. Either way, we are here now, almost all of us, and it may get really tough for us, but the ending will be great, no matter which way it turns out. You see, either we leave this old world struggling as it is and go on to our Heaven, our families, or we take down that monster in the fairytale and make the kingdom a better place... maybe. Better either way, right?" Jaz nodded.

"I have a question for you. When did you get so positive about life?" Cheater cast a puzzled frown his way.

"Hmm... I don't know. I guess my little sister rubbed off on me some," he replied, a smile lighting his face. "Hey, that new kid's waking up. Why don't you go help Lena with him. He's liable to pass out again when he sees her standing over him," Jaz joked.

"Truth!" Cheater nodded as she made her way to the couch. "Hey, Simon! Feeling better? Up to some food and water maybe?"

Simon's gaze moved from Lena to Cheater, then scanned the living room ceiling, "What happened? Who are you?" He asked Lena.

"Well, that's a first. You must not be completely with us yet. The first question most people ask me is 'How tall are you?'" Lena laughed.

"That was my next question," Simon added as Carmen brought him some soup and water.

Cheater helped Simon sit up.

Nathan joined them, "Why is it the new guy always gets all the girls?" His comment brought laughter throughout the two rooms. "Let me take a look at the bump."

"He needs some ice on it!" Carmen ordered.

"I got something a little better than ice!" Nathan smiled at her then sat next to Simon, placing both hands on the back of Simon's head as he sipped his soup.

"Need some help?" Rebecca asked, handing

Lena a sandwich.

The light behind Simon's head was the only answer she needed. Nathan's power was strong and something told her it would be necessary as their mission progressed.

John turned his eyes from the rearview mirror, blinked, and looked again. Had he seen something behind him? He glanced at Neka's concerned expression. "What's wrong?" She peered over her shoulder.

John looked at the mirror, again. "Nothing. I just... I thought I saw something, that's all."

Neka frowned at the driver who kept glancing in the mirror. She gave the backseat another quick look, paying attention to the darkness through the back window, shrugged. "Just go!" She ordered.

"Okay." John pulled the car away from the curb, drove slowly up the main street and took a left. The woods to his left danced with shadows from the street lights and the headlights as he picked up speed. Every few seconds he gave the rearview mirror a check which made Neka wary. An uncomfortable feeling grew in the pit of her stomach. "Why do you keep looking behind us? Is somebody supposed to be back there? Following us? Are you setting me up?" Her voice rose with anger at the thought of being double crossed.

"No, I'm not setting you up. It's just—nothing. I guess I'm paranoid enough that I'm seeing things. I swore I saw something back there before we left."

Neka's brows drew together in a neat V above her nose. Her eyes crinkled in a knowing smile. She turned her face to the window, a slight smile returned in her reflection.

Nashota and his games! She shook her head.

Returning her eyes to the road before them, she asked, "How far is it?"

"A few miles out of town. I'm just not sure this is a good idea. I mean, if he wants us all together, should we give him what he wants?"

"But you won't stay, right? I mean, you said you were going to stay with the force, see what he— whoever *he* is— is up to, so technically you won't be there, right? Plus, how do we even know the rest are there?"

"Yeah. Yeah, that's a good point. I still wish I knew what was going to happen, what he had planned. I know he's looking for something, I just don't know what. The others must be close, though, if he's pulling back one the search.

"Hey, do you still have that pendant I handed to you?"

Neka had forgotten about it. She felt her pocket, "Yes, and the paper."

"Don't lose it. I know he's looking for the pendants, all the rest of them. We each have one and he needs them for some reason."

"We do?" Neka asked.

"Yeah, I mean, I thought we did. That's what I was told from above."

"By who?" Neka wondered.

"Wait! Are you saying you don't have a pendant? A teardrop pendant your mother left you?"

A memory... a twirl... a flash of something dangling from a chain at her mother's throat. Where was it now? "No, but I remember her wearing one."

"Then he probably already has yours. And... I don't know how many of the others he possibly has, but it could be dangerous for us. I'm taking a big risk giving that one to you, so make sure you keep it safe. They'll know who I am if they find out I gave it to you, but we can't risk *him* getting it."

Thinking of her mother brought a pang of sadness. Where was she? Was she okay? And what about her father? They left that day and never came home, no news, no word. Then those police officers came. They wanted to take her and Nashota to CPS to place them in a foster home while they investigated, but nobody wanted to care for twin teens. They'd been separated for a few days, but

Nashota found her, as always, and they left together. They'd been on the run ever since, searching for that place, Paradise. She never wanted to be apart from Nashota, again. Deep down, her gut ached because she knew she would never again see her parents. Tears burned and she stiffened her spine to stop them.

John felt her mood change, saw her stiffen from the corner of his eye, felt the tension build in the air. He knew what she was thinking about, and he knew what happened to her parents. He was there. How could he tell her that, though?

He was there when her parents died, and even though he didn't take part in their disappearance, he saw the pictures, saw what happened, the evil the force brought upon them. His position allowed him to know everything about Neka and Nashota. Remembering that night created an ache in his abdomen, a lump grew in the pit of his stomach. He would have to tell her eventually, but how did he tell her? Would he want to know if he were her? Should he even tell her the truth?

A heavy silence filled the car during the remainder of the ride. Making the right turn into the driveway was like a habit for John. He'd been to this house numerous times. Once, shortly before he'd been promoted as an officer. He had come out with the cleanup crew. He'd never vomited so much in his life. That's when he learned just how evil the boss was, what tasks he would command to get what he wanted.

John had made up his mind then to do what he had to do... to learn everything about the man who'd had his family murdered. He hadn't expected to learn the truth about his own family, though.

What if, like Neka, he didn't know what had happened to his own family, who he really was?

A deep sigh escaped his lips. He killed the headlights and maneuvered the car to the back of the house. Keeping his foot on the brake pedal, he laid his arm over the back of the seat and faced Neka. "Go in. They'll look after you and your brother when he shows up. I'm going back to my official role. Tell them about me, that I'm working on the inside, for the man who set this all in motion. My phone number is on that piece of paper. Keep it safe. And if you need to call me, don't use the house phone. And whatever you do, keep that pendant out of sight."

"Why? What's so important about it?" Neka tilted her head.

"We'll know soon enough. Just keep it safe. Never leave it behind, and *don't* lose it."

Neka spoke the words before she realized it was the wrong time for jokes, "Does this mean we're exclusive? A couple? Engaged?" Her smile faded when she realized how the facetiousness of her words sounded in contrast to his sullen mood. No doubt another lecture was coming.

John's lip raised in a half smile. He shook his head and glanced toward the house. When he faced her, his features turned to concern. "We're about to go through some pretty rough stuff. Whatever happens, don't let it change you. I was a little hard on you before, when you came out of the barn, I know. But I had to get your attention, make you listen. You were in danger." He smiled at her and her heart flipped. "Go!"

Neka felt the urge to kiss him, but she resisted and pushed open the door. Her body shook with fear as she moved toward the house. When she heard the tires crunch on the gravel, she spun, longing to run back to the safety of the car and him. Was this a setup? Who was inside the house?

"Ugh! You don't need him. You have me! You'll always have me, Sis. Come on!" Nashota stood at her side.

"Thank goodness for that! You shouldn't have pulled that on him... in the backseat? You scared him!"

"What's a brother for? Besides, I felt the need for a test." He whistled a tune as he led her up the steps on the back porch.

"Again with the whistling? You may as well shout 'Hey, we're here!'"

"They already know." Nashota shrugged and walked through the door. Neka pulled open the screen door and turned the knob on the door that opened into the kitchen. Tentatively she stepped through. Splash met her and licked the dangling fingers of her left hand. Absently, she stroked his head in response as she craned her neck toward the living room. "Hello?" She whispered. Nobody responded. There wasn't anybody here. "Hello?" she repeated a little louder. What was Nashota talking about?

It couldn't be a trap. Nashota was already inside, though she didn't see him. He would have warned her if it were... Suddenly Nashota appeared before her.

"Nobody's here. Is it a trap? Do you think John set a trap for us?" Neka moved to the center of the kitchen.

Splash followed her, nosing her fingers asking for more attention.

"She can't be bad. Splash loves her," Rebecca silently suggested.

Neka—startled by the invisible commenter—stepped backward and for the doorknob. "Who said that?" Were they like Nashota? All of them? Could they hide themselves the way he did? "Where are you? Look, an officer brought me here. I don't know you, but he said to tell you that I am a Gifted One, whatever that means."

One by one the others appeared as they broke the link between them. "An officer?" Cai questioned. "What officer?"

"John. That's all I know. His name is John and he dropped me off and told me to tell you he is on the inside, working for the man who is behind all this, us, our lives... the man who destroyed our lives. That's all I know. He left me, and Nashota, here with you, said we would be safe and that he would contact us as he learns more about the plan? I don't know what he meant."

"Nashota? Who's that? Where is he?" Thad searched the kitchen.

"He hides, like you," Neka looked at Nashota. "Sometimes I can see him and others can't. Sometimes I can't even see him. He's here." She waved a hand toward her brother. "My name is Neka. My parents disappeared last year. We've been on our own since Nashota rescued me from the foster home I was in."

"Ugh! Foster homes! Don't mention them! I've seen enough of those," Cheater moved forward. "Come in!" She offered looking around the room. "Jaz, Rebecca, Nathan, Cai, Thad, Carmen, Simon, Jamie, Lena, and I am Cheater, well, Sarah." She held out her arms, "We are the Gifted Ones. You and Nashota make twelve. I guess we're all together, now.

Now what happens?"

"Good question, but I bet it's about to get real. Do we wait? Do we keep searching, and for what exactly?" Jaz wondered. "How long before they come after us?"

Wait! All together? Neka thought. *Did John lie to me? Is he not a Gifted One?*

Thad peered nervously at each of them, "Technically, there's only eleven. I don't see her brother, Na—?"

"Nashota!" Neka reminded him. "He's there! You can't see him? If I can see him, if John can see him, why can't you all see him?" She turned to Nashota, but he was gone again. "Ugh! He's not there... again." Neka mumbled under her breath, "Wild goose!"

"I'm sorry what did you say?" Jamie, closest to Neka and Cheater, asked as he did the math. If John was one of them, too...

That made thirteen. Each looked at Jamie, knowing his thoughts, then around Neka searching for Nashota, then the kitchen, and back at each other's confused expressions.

J ohn parked the car in its original spot, taking care to replace the key to its exact spot under the mat leaving everything as it was. He had a phenomenal memory, so much better than most, picture perfect. That was his gift, he guessed.

Closing the car door carefully so as not to alert anyone in the house, he eased away from the car and began his long walk home.

"Well, well, back to stealing cars I see." The crunch of tires rolling up next to him stiffened his spine.

John froze at the stop sign as the car stopped. He knew the voice, and he cringed every time he heard it.

"So, how'd it go?"

John thought about lying, but he knew it wouldn't do any good. Without his pendant, he was left wide open and couldn't trust anyone at work. He would have to really get into his role now.

"Great! Dropped them off just as requested. They're all together now. All twelve of them."

"Good, get in. Boss wants to meet you. He has something special for you to do since that Indian chick took such a shine to you."

John blacked his mind. *Nothing. Think about nothing. Nothing but blackness, darkness. Nothing at all.* His spine popped as he straightened further, "Sure." He moved behind the car to the passenger side watching the taillights as he passed. He wouldn't put anything past this man. Safely making it to the door, he pulled the handle and seated himself. Tugging the seatbelt from right to left, he snapped it in place.

"Seat belt? Really? Since when?" The driver's stare sent a shiver down his spine.

"Hey, I'm an officer of the law, right? Lead by example and all that crap!" John threw in a manly chuckle to conceal his real feelings.

"You are one strange kid. I bet you were bullied to no end when you were little. What the hell is so special about you that you are one of us? What can you do that I can't do? Why did the boss take to you the way he did? Tell me!" The driver ordered as he checked the intersecting street for traffic before making his turn.

"I don't know what I did." But John did know the truth.

"Huh. Couldn't be that you're like... family?"

John's tension rose. Nobody knew. How did he find out? Did everyone on the force know? The fear became reality. He was finally going to meet the man who brought him to this place in his life. He was finally going to meet the one who sent for him when he was younger, his estranged uncle, the one who hated his family so much that he had them killed. He was coming face to face with the monster who destroyed everything in his path, every person who loved and trusted him, every city he'd led. He was coming face to face with the man in his nightmares.

"Does that scare ya' kid? Us knowin' the truth about you? That scare ya'? 'Cause it should." The driver sneered as he floored the gas pedal climbing the speed up beyond the limit. Faster the car sped up the highway to the unknown location of John's uncle as the nearer John grew to his fear, his nightmare, maybe his death.

He glanced at the driver, his twisted grinning face as oncoming headlights lit his features. John could see the potential for playing chicken with those oncoming cars. He could see the risk this man would take to please his uncle. The man was psycho. John questioned whether or not his meeting with his estranged uncle would take place at all. From the look of the cop next to him, this would be John's last few minutes of life.

He couldn't believe the force all knew.

He was in danger beyond that of his dream, of their dream, the Gifted Ones.

Tonight—he was certain—he would die.

"Come on, kid! You're a little young to be on the force. You didn't think we'd figure it out? Hell, you're still wet behind the ears. But tonight, you ain't gonna get any older!"

John swallowed hard and stared at his lap. He thought about Neka, beautiful Neka, and her brother. Had Nashota made it to the house? He never saw him, except that silhouette in the mirror. Was that him? What power he had to hide himself that way!

John would never see Neka, again. He hoped the Gifted Ones could handle what was to come.

"Yeah, she was a purty one, huh?" The driver began to laugh at John. John's face grew hot with rage. He gritted his teeth, angry breaths flaring his nostrils. His head came up, "Look out!" He crossed his arms in front of his face.

A man stood in the middle of their lane on the highway.

The driver slammed on the brakes, pulled the wheel to the right, and cut it left in the ditch to gain traction, but the loose gravel kept the car on a straight path to a tree that impacted the driver's front fender. An air bag pushed John's arms into his face. He tasted blood from his upper lip. His arms, neck, and back hurt from the impact, but his side of the car was left untouched by the accident.

The passenger door opened from the outside and a hand gripped John's right arm. "Come on out. Called 911. You'll be fine."

John looked up through swelling eyes, but the one who had helped him was gone. Where? Who was it?

Darkness filled John's vision and his body crumbled beside the cop car.

John woke up in a hospital room uncertain how long he'd been there.

A card on the bed tray was the first thing he noticed. Stiffly he moved to lift it.

John

Nothing else on the front. The envelope was unsealed. Carefully he separated the two ends of the card to check inside. Just writing.

He pulled it free from the envelope to reveal the cover

Get Well Soon

You did good kid. Proud of you. I was going to have him removed from the force anyway. Heal quickly. We'll finally meet after all this time. I will protect you from my followers. Don't worry. We have too much to do together for me to risk losing you.

Uncle J.

John closed the card, tentatively placing it back into the envelope. A tear escaped the corner of his eye.

Why didn't I just die? He thought.

Death would be better than what he had to face, the planned betrayal, the fate of Neka.

How did his uncle know about the plan to kill him? Was that him in front of the car? Was it he who had stopped the car? How could he do that? The powers he must already have, powers he'd stolen from them, powers stolen from betrayed love, powers turned to greed, hate, murder!

John closed his eyes to the sound of beeps and buzzes coming from a room down the hall. "We lost him!" A doctor shouted. "Better let the boss know."

"Ouch!" Jamie drew back his finger.

"What is it? What happened?" Lena looked over his shoulder as he shook his hand before squeezing the tip of his right index finger. "Sliver."

"Yikes! Batman has a sliver? Is it like kryptonite?"

"Wrong superhero," Jamie rolled his eyes. "Give me a hand so we can get this board loose."

Crowbar in hand, Lena pried the tip into a gap between two weathered boards and pulled with all her strength to pop the top of the board loose. "I don't know what we are supposed to be looking for, but I sure hope we find it soon. My arms are getting sore."

"I didn't know farms could have so many buildings hidden on them." Cai grinned at Nathan.

"What do you think it is? I mean, the thing they want, what we're looking for?" Neka glanced at the others working at taking down boards as she moved beyond them to peer through another crack. If

Nashota were here, she could get in. Where was he?

The board Lena pried on finally popped free from the wall, "Got it!" Carmen shined a flashlight into the darkness. Another empty space.. it was just another building with nothing inside, like all the others. Why were all of the buildings empty? This was a farm. Didn't farms have equipment?

As she pulled the flashlight back from the opening, the light flickered across the ceiling. Something in that brief wave of light was familiar to Carmen. "Wait!" She shoved the flashlight back through the opening and directed it to the ceiling; she bent forward at the waist and angled her head to get a better view. Simon stood behind her trying to look inside over her head.

"Holy..." Simon's jaw went slack.

"Crap!" Carmen finished. "It's the spiral! This must be the place!"

"What spiral? What are you talking about?" Several voices questioned as they moved nearer, taking turns to peer into the building.

"This has to be it, what we're looking for," Lena added quietly.

"What do we do now?" Cheater asked.

"Tear down this door! Make an opening. Let's get in there and see what the big deal is!" Jaz answered.

"But, what if *they* are still looking for this

place, too? There weren't any tire tracks around, nobody has driven to this location. What if they didn't find it when they were here, and they've just been waiting for us to find it?" Nathan pointed out. "Maybe they're watching right now." Nathan whispered suspiciously.

"Right." Simon nodded. "Maybe we should act like it's just another empty building. Walk away. We could come back later. We'll need an opening we can get through and cover back up so they won't know how to get into this building. If Nathan has nails, Carmen's pretty good at building things."

Carmen punched Simon on the arm, "Yeah, outta cardboard boxes, plastic and newspapers!" She corrected him.

They laughed. "Simon's right. We need to be able to get in there and seal it back up from the inside. For now, let's put this board back up, and go to another building. We'll take down the boards at the other buildings to make it look like this one. That way they won't know we found anything. Then, we can come back here and fix the hole up so it looks like it's still closed up, but with an opening big enough for us to get through." Cai tugged the loose board back into place and moved to the left of Lena while Jaz hammered it up.

Later that night when they returned to the dilapidated barn, eleven teens slipped through the opening to prepare a fake wall in the barn. Pulling the makeshift door into place, they followed the flashlight beams to the center of the barn. The place was completely empty. Nothing hung on the walls, no equipment rested on the dirt floor.

"Hey, did you hear that? Put out the light!" Rebecca froze.

Splash squeezed through a low opening where the dogs had burrowed beneath to make a hole. The farm dogs followed him.

"Whew!" Carmen let out her breath and moved forward before switching the light on. Above her, light spread and reflected from the spiral, as if she were under a spot light. "What the...?" She looked up.

"Don't move!" Thad panicked. "What if it's rigged somehow? Like if she moves it will blow up the barn and us, too?"

"You've got some imagination, Thad!" Cai tilted her head upward and moved around Carmen slowly. There was no need for the flashlight, so Carmen switched it off.

It had to be motion detected lighting. But who put it there? And why? Cai walked carefully outward around Carmen, stopping and catching her breath as a light fell on her. "I think they're meant for us. Each of us has a light. Watch! Thad, come here."

Cai pointed the others to positions beneath the spiral until each of them stood beneath a cone of light devised to switch on when a certain one of them stood below it. Eleven teens stood beneath eleven cones of light. Eleven lights glowed downward creating a spiral of inverted light funnels, encasing each in sparkling dust swirls.

Eleven?

"Where's Nashota?" Cai turned to Neka who glanced around the dark barn beyond the lit spiral. She hadn't noticed the halt of whistling. She hadn't noticed Nashota's absence. When had he disappeared?

"I don't know," She shrugged.

"Don't you have some kind of control over that brother of yours?" Lena shook her head.

"Eh, not really. He's my twin, but he's always been an exact opposite of me." Neka peered toward the moonlight shining around and through the cracks in the walls.

"Nothing's happening," Simon looked up. "Except all this glowing dust." He waved his hand into the dust watching the pieces part temporarily where he placed his hand, as if polar opposites, and then the dust returned to the circling flow of its destination.

"I wouldn't say nothing, but yeah, nothing else. Nothing that would answer any questions." Nathan nodded, following the upward gaze of the others.

"It must take twelve. We'll have to come back. Hey look!"

One by one the names of the Gifted Ones appeared in the lights above their head, Cheater, Jaz, Rebecca, Nathan, Carmen, Simon, Cai— Thad jumped out of the light before his name could display above his head. "There! There goes Nashota!" Thad lied and ran through the opening.

Neka watched him leave. She frowned. Did he see Nashota or did he have a secret? She watched the others as they followed one by one. Neka glanced up at the light Thad had been standing under. The faint glow dissipated as she squinted to see the name, but there was nothing.

"Where'd he go? Nashota! Come back! We found something," Thad whispered harshly.

Nashota appeared next to his sister inside the barn.

"Did you..." she began.

"Nope. It's not me they're looking for. I've been standing here the whole time."

"Why didn't you come stand in your place?" Neka moved out of the light, hands on hips.

He shrugged, "I thought I was. Maybe there's

only room for one spotlight in our family, Wild Goose."

"What? Don't call me that! You're the wild goose! How are we supposed to know what happens if you won't cooperate?" Neka moved to the opening looking left and right for the others.

"We know where it is, now. That's all we need to know. I have a feeling there's something more important for us to learn before we figure all this out." Nashota's chin lifted in the direction of the others. "Come on." He moved through the wall next to Neka.

When Nashota remained undiscovered by the others, they sealed up the hole and left for the house. Not understanding Nashota's absence, though they'd never actually seen him before, their spirits were low. They'd been looking for days for the right building, for answers, and now that they had found the building, they felt they knew less than before.

"Man! I really wanted to light up that spiral. I mean, what else can we do with these powers of ours. We must have something to do with that spiral. We turned our lights on, right?" Nathan kicked at dirt with the toe of his shoe. "What's wrong with that crazy brother of yours? And how come the rest of us haven't seen him?"

Neka reached around the back of her head to pull long, black glistening hair to her left shoulder. It was warming up for December. "Look, I don't know. Maybe there's something we need to know before we can figure it all out. Maybe it has to do with one of us." She raised her brows at Thad who'd been watching her since they left.

He swallowed hard, his hand shuffling something in his pocket. Neka frowned, watched his movements, then turned her attention back to the others. "Maybe one of us has a secret that the others don't know."

"That's not likely... we all know what the others are thinking thanks to Jaz." Cai playfully punched Jaz in the arm.

"Hey, you know what? I think I'm gonna run up ahead! Anybody up for racing back to the house! Loser has to do the dishes tonight!" Thad burst into a sprint as Neka raised her head in curiosity.

"Sh... You're on!" Nathan nodded catching Thad easily.

"If we don't race, we don't have to do the dishes, right?" Rebecca patted Splash's head.

"Sounds good to me," Lena smiled. "I'll walk. When I run, earthquakes follow. Besides, I'm like a bad juggling act when it comes to doin' dishes. And... running in the dark? Nah! No, thank you!"

Rebecca smiled.

"Good morning, John! How are you feeling?" The shift nurse appeared by his side. John squinted into the light. His head hurt. "Doctor's coming by to check on you, then you're outta here. Nothing serious." Her long blond ponytail fell over her right shoulder as she checked the chart. She raised her eyes to his with a twinkling look of recognition. "Feeling okay?"

"Yeah, I'm fine. Let me guess, you're on his payroll, too?"

Innocence filled her features, "Whose payroll? I get paid by the hospital like any other nurse." Her grin answered his question. "And... to answer your next question: yes, I was here last night when you arrived." She checked his pulse sending an electrical charge up his arm. She was dangerous alright.

"Thought so. I remember your hair and those eyes," John turned on the charm.

"Huh," she raised her brows. "If you weren't so much younger than I..."

"What's age got to do with anything?" John flirted back.

"Well, you're awake! Good, about time to go home. Let's see here..." The doctor took the chart from his nurse, "Mhm, mhm, vitals look good. Let's check those eyes." Flash of light right, flash left. "Looks good, looks good. How're you feeling?"

"Great! A little sleepy." John nodded.

"Yes, you had a rough night there. Well, let's send you home for some rest. Won't have any two hour wake ups tonight. Nurse, set up his discharge, please."

"Yes Doctor!" She winked at the patient.

"You can get dressed now. I'll close the door. Be careful out there, son. It's a dangerous world." The doctor exited the room leaving behind a thick blanket of fear.

Was that a threat? Did I just get threatened by a doctor? John pushed up to a sitting position on the bed. He watched the doctor swing the door closed behind him no longer certain who could be trusted.

When had his position leaked to the lower level leaders and cops? When the meeting was scheduled?

John felt danger. He needed a safe place to wait. The only safe place he could be sure of, the only people he could trust, were the Gifted Ones. But if he went to them, they would all be together... And that's what his uncle wanted. If that's what *he* wanted, then they would all be in danger.

There had to be someplace else... someone else he could trust to hide him from his uncle's entourage. Who though? There were no friends, no adults, there was nobody. Maybe he *should* head out to the farm, try to get Neka's attention. She could help hide him. There were many buildings on that property. He knew because he searched them all with the force. At that time, his uncle was searching for the pendants. Now he was waiting until the Gifted Ones all joined together on the farm for the final piece of their mission, the final piece of the prophecy. What had the Captain of the force said *he* wanted from them? Their powers, but for what?

What was it? What was he up to?

John opened the closet door. Hanging there were clean jeans, a clean shirt, all the necessities of a fresh new day. After removing the clothes from the hanger, he felt the pockets. He squeezed every seam and hem, feeling every square inch of every article of clothing, finding nothing.

Next he picked up the new shoes, pulling up the lining, checking for cracks in the soles, anywhere a tracking device could have been planted.

Nothing... he found no bugs or devices that would track his movement. Not one hem held embedded wires or tiny buttons. His head spun with the danger of his situation, and the irony. He didn't know who was on which side anymore. Perhaps the faction brought these clothes to him. Some of the faction on the inside had infiltrated the force in anticipation of intervening for the Gifted Ones. Hopefully it was the faction. They knew the consequences of a failed mission and they had joined to make sure the twelve didn't fail. How many new members did they have now? John had been asked to keep his distance for the sake of the operation and only received messages when necessary.

How many may have turned? Could he trust anyone at the hospital at all? And what if any of the upper level faction had turned and were playing dual roles? His uncle was a powerful and persuasive man, so he'd heard.

John knew of at least two of the faction that had turned because he'd accidentally overheard some of his uncle's men talking while they searched the vast outbuildings of the farm for the teens. At that time, that's what his uncle wanted to know, where the teens were, whether any had arrived yet.

And when the first two teens arrived, he'd set his trap for the others to draw the rest to the farm.

Who else can I turn to? John pulled the door open a sliver and glanced both ways down the hall before spotting the nurse's nod of safe exit. He slipped down the hall, spotted the lost and found desk, and inquired about his blue hoodie, size large.

"Oh, yes, we have it right here!" The candy striper pulled the folded jacket from the shelf below.

John almost laughed at the simplicity wondering how many blue hoodies they acquired weekly.

He rounded a corner scanning for cameras and staff.

Nobody.

He pulled the hoodie over his head; the hood hung low enough to shade his features. Next he located a supply closet, dug some scrub bottoms and shoe covers from the waste can, and pulled them over his own clothing and sneakers.

When he was certain he was disguised, he exited the hospital through the emergency doors, casually headed to the apartment building across the street, hands buried deep in the hoodie pockets, hunched slightly forward to hide his features, and slipped inside the building, just another intern going home to his lonely apartment for a nap.

"**N**eka! Neka! The truth must be told. You know the truth. See it. Tell the others before it's too late. He's coming for you, Neka. All of you!"

Neka had been tossing in her sleep, each time waking and dozing off again, but this last dream awakened her.

An icy sweat kissed her forehead and she sat up wrapping herself in a shivering embrace, rubbing her arms for warmth. Even the touch of Cheater's calf to hers did not bring warmth.

Her mother's voice. Again, her mother reached out to her in her dreams talking about the truth. *What truth, Mom?*

Briefly, she thought about Thad, the pendant in her own pocket wrapped in a note, Thad's hand in his pocket, his quick changes. She glanced at her jeans hanging over the chair. It was the first time she'd taken them off before going to sleep. It was the first time in a long time she'd felt safe enough to sleep like a regular girl.

She wondered about John. Was he safe? He had saved her and her brother. Where was he, now? She didn't even know if they could trust him. Was he the twelfth Gifted One? Was Thad a traitor?

The truth? Is that what Mom wanted me to see, that one of them was a traitor?

She'd been here three days with the Gifted Ones. She'd been here all that time and not talked about John since the first night. All three nights her mother warned her of the truth, and then again, tonight.

"He's coming for me... us," She whispered.

Cheater sensed Neka waking up and wiped her eyes clear of sleep. "Okay, I'm guessing your mother again, right? But what is she talking about? The truth? What do you have against Thad? I mean, yeah, he's been acting strange since we arrived, but what do you know that you haven't told us?"

Neka turned wide eyes on Cheater. "I should admit, we've been a little nervous about you because we haven't seemed to join with you like we have the others. I mean, we know each other's every thought, every dream, every emotion and word; we share powers, but you, your thoughts are scattered and dreams are few. Now this dream? Again? Who exactly are you, Neka? Who's coming for you?"

Cai pushed open the bedroom door and

stepped in, next Rebecca and Carmen. The boys offering to crash in the living room, minus Nashota who had not yet made an appearance in the three days since John had dropped them off.

"What's all the noise? Is something happening?" Carmen yawned, stretching her arms toward the ceiling. "It's too early."

"I'm not sure, but there may be a traitor among us," Cheater had left the bed and moved closer to the others, eyes on Neka.

"No! I can explain! I should have told you already, but— I don't know why I didn't."

She rose from the bed, reaching for her jeans.

"Wait!" Cai beat her to the folded pants on the chair and hugged them to her chest. "What do you have? What's so important about them? You're wearing pajamas." Cai backed toward the others as Cheater closed the bedroom door, shutting the girls in. Cai patted the pockets, found the wrapped pendant and removed it.

"Please! I'm not a traitor! I just... I don't always make the best decisions, that's all. Yes, my mother warned me the past three nights." Neka turned to Cheater in the dimly lit room, streaks of moonlight filtering onto the latter's face. "She's been trying to warn me, but I don't know what she means. The pendant, it's not mine, not my mother's. John gave it to me to hold onto..." Here it was, the time for truth.

Is this what her mother meant?

A knock at the door interrupted Neka's thoughts. "Hey! Am I missin' somethin'?" Lena eased the door open and ducked her head beneath the frame to peer into the dimly lit room. "Need some lights!" She reached with her large hand to flip the switch behind Cai's head.

Everyone in the room blinked against the brightness.

"What's goin' on?" The guys filtered upstairs.

"Not so fast there, guys!" Lena blocked the door.

"I guess we're getting up, now?" Carmen yawned and sighed. "Ugh! We'll meet you guys downstairs."

"Yeah, it seems like somebody in this room has something to tell us all," Cai added.

Neka lowered her head. Why was she always getting herself into trouble? Where was Nashota when she needed him to help her out of trouble this time? Where had he gone?

"Okay, wait. So this John... he's one of us, too?" Simon placed hands on hips. "That makes thirteen, so that means..."

"There's only twelve in the story," Rebecca reminded him.

"Exactly!" The rest replied in unison turning toward Neka.

"Look, I don't know the answer! I've done the math and I've been wondering the same thing you are now. Is John telling me the truth?"

"Or, is it Nashota? We have yet to see him." Jaz peered around the room and shrugged at the others.

"Of course Nashota is one of us! He is! He's my twin brother. If he weren't, then I wouldn't be either!"

"Alright, so what about this?" Cai dangled the necklace before Neka. "Is this some kind of tracking device or something? What is it? Why is it so important?"

The look Neka gave Thad was not lost on anyone in the room and they all turned to Thad.

Cai moved into Thad's personal space, face to face with the young man she thought of as a brother, "What do you know?" Sensing nothing from him, her eyes followed the length of his right arm to the hand hidden in his pants pocket.

"Stop!" Thad stepped back away from her hand. "It's mine. I'll take it out!" His hand slipped from his pocket and from his fingertips dangled an identical pendant.

"Where'd you get that?" Nathan moved closer.

"Like her, it was my mom's." Thad nodded

toward Neka. "She told me to keep it secret when she gave it to me. She said it... it blocked... it made..."

"Thoughts? Made you normal?" Cheater's look of betrayal sent a shiver down Thad's spine.

"She told me to keep it secret. My mother..." Tears blurred Thad's vision.

"And you've been using it to block your thoughts from us? The truck ride? Since we've been here? How long have you had it?" Cai quizzed. "You," she turned to Neka, "you I can understand. You don't know us. But you," she turned back to Thad, "you?" Pain of betrayal filled her eyes.

"I'm not a traitor!" Thad yelled before running out the front door into the predawn darkness.

"I'll go after him!" Jaz turned to follow.

"No!" Handing the pendant back to Neka, Cai pushed open the screen door and disappeared.

"Great! Now I don't know who to trust!" Carmen eyed them all, hands on hips. "I thought those people were bringing me someplace safe. Man! I'm outta here!" She took the stairs two at a time to collect her belongings.

"No, stop! There is a way we can find out the truth!" Cheater called, stopping Carmen on the landing. Carmen turned slowly.

"We've been so caught up in figuring out what was here, what the men who took over the farm were looking for, that none of us have had a reason to contact our mothers and ask the questions we have," Cheater shrugged, elbows bent, palms up.

"We can talk to our mothers? Wait, I can talk to my mom?" Neka, Carmen, Simon, Jamie and Lena asked in unison.

"Yes, we can. We can talk to all of them. We can learn the truth about everything," Cheater smiled at Jaz.

"Yeah, we can. Well, we can when Thad and Cai return. Do you think we can bring them here... our mothers... together? At once?" Jaz asked.

"Well, eleven of them maybe," Cheater frowned.

"There's only eleven of us right now, and doing that would help us determine who is not one of us," Rebecca reminded.

Suspicion shadowed their joy as they searched the wary faces around them.

"Thad, stop! What is wrong with you?" Cai stretched her arm forward, stumbling as she grabbed Thad's elbow. She balanced herself before spinning him to face her. "What is your problem?"

"I... I don't know. I didn't want to tell you... anyone. I don't know... I just... I don't trust them."

"Them? And by them, you mean me? How can

you say that? Who do you trust then? *Him?* The faceless creature in our nightmare? The man who did this to you? To us?" Cai shook him hard, releasing his elbow from her grasp in disgust. "If you truly are not a traitor, then come back to the house. Sort this out. Tell the truth. If you are, this is your chance to walk away unharmed before I beat the crap outta you!"

Thad took a deep breath, looked at the toes of his shoes as he exhaled, then faced Cai. How could he tell her? How could he trust her?

"You don't trust me. Okay, go!" She turned toward the house, "and don't ever come near me, again."

Thad stared at the middle of her back until she was twenty feet away. He had to stay. He couldn't leave now. "Wait!"

Cai stopped, but she didn't turn around.

Thad stepped cautiously toward her, "Wait, please. I didn't mean to hurt you. I'll tell you everything... or, what I know anyway."

"I can't believe you, Thad! After all the time I've protected you."

"Yeah, well, my dad protected me, too... once." Shame filled his eyes, and the look softened Cai's heart. The big sister to the little brother she had grown to care about, "Come on. You might as well explain to everyone."

"Listen to me! Things are getting really bad here. America won't be the same. We will leave for the Middle East next week! That's final!"

"I'm not leaving my home, my family. What about Thad's schooling? He's in one of the best private schools available. No, we won't go. You go if you are so afraid of what is coming, but I won't." Thad listened through his bedroom door to his parents' argument. With his back to the door, he stared out his window as the argument continued. His mother was right. Thad didn't want to go to his father's birthplace. Of course, his school wasn't all his mother thought it was. If they were to ask Thad, he would tell them it was a waste of their money. He wasn't learning anything of value. Most days he felt brain-washed into believing ideals against his heartfelt beliefs. Just yesterday, their test had been over some new societal changes coming that would ruin America's democracy. His classmates agreed with the positives presented by their teacher, but Thad saw the whole picture. Thad saw the truth behind the lies. He said so in his essay question. He knew the teacher would fail him, but he didn't care. He was a freak to his classmates.

The tone of his father's voice rose significantly,

pulling Thad back to the present. His mother's voice matched tones and then her scream forced Thad to spin around, reach for the doorknob, and slip quietly down the hallway to...

To what? He had thought. I can't go against my dad. He's hit me before and he's much larger than I am. What am I doing?

His mother screamed again just before another sound much worse than a slap, this time there was a thud, and her voice fell silent.

Thad burst into the living room where his mother lay crumpled at the fireplace, blood staining the rug below her head.

"What did you do?" Thad screamed at his father before running to his mother's side.

Thad felt his father's strong fingers grip his shoulder, but the movement was controlled, somewhat comforting. "It was an accident son. Go! Pack your clothes. We are leaving this country tonight."

"We have to call 911. Get help! Mother will die!" A tear dropped from Thad's cheek onto his mother's arm as he knelt by her side.

"She is already gone. Go! Go now! Pack your things!" His father's grip tightened as his tone grew firm.

"No! We have to get help!" Thad stood and whirled to face his father just as his father's open hand met Thad's cheek.

"*Do as you're told or suffer the same fate as your mother!*"

"*Yes, Father,*" *Thad lowered his eyes in respect. Feeling the heat of the slap on his cheek with his own hand, the young man turned down the hall toward his room. Halfway there, his world changed, he lost the present moment and felt a strong wind within the house.*

Thad returned to the present and found himself in an alley a few blocks from his home. Puzzled by the change, he stumbled weakly back to the address of his house and found his home scattered throughout the neighborhood, bits here, boards there, roof tiles in trees, bricks in neighbors' yards, and at the center was the concrete foundation as if the house had exploded from inside out.

"**W** here is he?"

"Sir, I'm sorry. We lost him at the hospital. The cameras, there's nobody coming out of the hospital with those clothes on. We haven't found him, yet."

"Did he take the phone? Have you tried the GPS?" His voice rose in anger.

"Apparently, it's not on. We tried tracking it."

"Somebody must have seen him somewhere. Something isn't right about this, him disappearing now. If I could connect with him, speak telepathically to him... if I only had that girl's power. How did the force learn who he was?" His accusing eyes burned into those of his third ranking assistant. The younger man stood his ground. He didn't even blink.

"I don't know sir." Inside the man quivered, yet his words were steady, strong. "We'll keep looking, Sir. Sir?"

"What is it now?" The angry outburst shook the office.

"There's rumors, and I'm sure that's all they are, that a faction of non believers has infiltrated our precincts."

"If it's a damn rumor, then why are you bringing it up? You're wasting time! Gather the men at the usual meeting place. I want to talk to them. I will find my nephew!" Fists pounded the mahogany desk before him as he spun his chair to face the window. The roiling cloud filled sky beyond the window brought a sneer to his lips as he breathed, "Damn those kids!"

"But sir, what if the rumor is true?" The assistant pressed.

"Raghrrr!" The man in black threw his head back in frustration. "I need those powers! We can no longer wait for them to unite. We must unite them, force them together. With their powers, I will know who is with us and who isn't. Gather the men to the meeting place."

"Yessir." The assistant backed out of the office pulling the door closed behind him. Beads of sweat formed on his forehead and he wiped them away with the back of his hand. His chest deflated a relieved sigh.

Where could the nephew be? The faction did not have him. Which of the other LOD's might have him? Was it possible that he slipped away on his own? Why? Unless that was his solution to keeping the twelve apart... Of course! Yes, he was a smart one.

The dispatcher's office was on the second floor. He'd sent cryptic messages so many times that he knew exactly how to word the message to the faction without tipping off the LOD's. The elevator opened and he nodded to the three officers, "Morning, officers."

Three grunts followed his greeting.

The doors slid closed.

A strong arm slipped around his throat before he could fight them off. A gun stabbed his rib cage. "Where is he?"

"He, who?" Though calm words brought pain to his strained vocal cords, his heart thumped heavily within.

"The nephew... we lost a good man last night because of him. Where is the kid?" The harsh words and hot breath in his ear raised the hair on the back of his neck. The feeling produced a memory of a mountain lion spying him in the hayfield on his grandparents' property when he was fourteen. He could feel the lion there because his hair raised the same way, but he never saw it.

"I'm sure I don't know who you are talking about. If you would, please push the number two. I'm headed to dispatch to call the troops in for a meeting. You might want to join us. You should probably ask *him* about *the nephew*, whoever that is. Of course, if he doesn't hear the message he wants sent, he'll send someone to figure out why."

Another grunt fell into his ear.

The gun slid away from his side as the arm eased away from his neck.

The elevator began its descent to the second floor.

"Thank you, gentlemen." He tugged at his coat tails and straightened his tie. "Have a safe day out there." A calm smile and nod as the elevator doors closed satisfied the officers' suspicions about what he knew.

After the doors slid closed, he moved quickly down the hall to dispatch where he collapsed into the extra chair.

"Rough morning?" The most beautiful brown eyes he'd ever seen glanced his way.

"You could say that. I don't know..." He shook his head uncertainly.

The ponytailed brunette reached over and patted his leg understanding his uncertainty. She'd known him for a long time. He'd gotten her onto the dispatch team, but she'd known him much longer than that.

"I honestly don't know how you do it. You have the hardest job on this team. I wouldn't want it!" She smiled at him.

He looked into her eyes and found love, fear,

hope. He married her for that love and hope all those years ago. She believed in him, in their cause, in the faction.

Drawing courage from her, he smiled. "I'm worried, but we have another message. Let's do this." A thin smile played on his lips before they carefully crafted the message she would send out to the force.

John huddled among the shadows in the woods laying low until nightfall. He knew the force was on the lookout for him. His back against the well hidden trunk of a tree, he lowered his forehead to his knees and closed his eyes, the scent of the sun filtered woodland forcing a memory.

John stood on the edge of the trailer as it bounced through the rough patches of the hayfield. His best friend, Zeke, stood opposite him, a stupid grin on his sweaty face. The temperatures in North Texas had soared to near a hundred degrees. This would be the last cut of hay before the summer months dried the hayfield to a golden brown. This was their last paid job of the season.

"Man! You can't be in love. You're sixteen! You just want one thing. You know that's why you feel that way!" Zeke shook his head at John's counter

argument before sending a shrill whistle to the pony-tailed brunette driving the truck, an indication for her to stop so they could load more hay bales onto the trailer.

Side by side bales brought the guys within earshot of each other. "Dude, I'm telling you... I am in love with her. I plan to marry that girl!"

John shook his head again, tossing the fifty pound bale of hay onto the trailer and moving to the other side of the trailer to lift another one. He tossed it up to Zeke, who had begun stacking the recent bales.

"Need some help?" The pretty brunette bounced out of the truck to pick up a bail even with the driver's door. She dropped it at John's feet for him to throw up. She was a beauty. John had to admit that. Her brown eyes were like chocolate and sparkled with mischief. She was slender, but wiry, strength in every curve of her muscles, and her curves were in all the right places. John could see why Zeke might "think" he was in love with her.

"Thanks," John nodded. He tossed the bail up to Zeke, who stood speechless, mouth dogged as he stuttered a few mumbled words. John turned away from the girl, a sheepish grin on his face as he shook his head at his best friend. He mouthed the word, "Loser."

"Uhm... Hey, Brandy! Would you... uhm, I mean..." Zeke stuttered.

Brandy tilted her head, shaded her eyes with her hand, and wrinkled her nose at Zeke. "I was thinking about grabbing some lunch and taking a swim when we finish here. Wanna join me?" Though her words fell innocently on Zeke's ears, John caught all the mischief in her attempt to save Zeke from complete and utter failure of his request.

John turned to Brandy, a knowing smile playing on his face.

"Oh, you can come to, John... if you really want to." Brandy emphasized the last phrase.

"Thanks, Brandy, but I'm pretty sure I have plans," John declined.

Brandy winked at John as Zeke stood above looking silly, "Not me! I don't have plans! Yeah, I could eat... and swim. Sounds great!"

"Great!" Brandy turned and walked back to the open door of the truck easily pulling herself up into the driver seat.

John wagged his head at his best friend, "Man, she is so much smoother than you."

"Shut up!" Zeke threatened to throw a bail down at John, then climbed off the stack to sit on the back of the trailer, his stupid grin filling his tanned features.

"John told me that each of our mothers had a pendant at one time. I don't know what is so important about them. He told me to keep it safe. The man he works for, the man behind this... everything that is happening... he took our pendants. I think that's the reason our parents are gone. I think the pendants..." Neka swung the pendant while she formed the words.

"Make us normal, or shield our powers or something like that." Thad added, his identical pendant in rhythm with hers. "I remembered— in the truck— what my mom told me when she gave it to me to hold onto for her. It was when my dad first approached her about leaving. Anyway, I tested it. I've been testing it since we left Maive's."

Almost in unison six of them rose. "Maive!" They'd forgotten the note, possibly her last words by now.

"Wait!" Cai ordered. "You've had the pendant

the entire time I've known you... since I found you in that alley?" She asked Thad.

"Yes." Shame filled Thad's eyes before he glanced away.

"Hang on, hang on!" Simon the unbiased newcomer jumped in. "Didn't you tell us about Thad rescuing some guy at a pizza place?"

"Yes," Cai nodded, the distrust leaving her features.

"All right, just, you know, give the guy a break." Simon patted Thad's shoulder.

"Thanks," Thad's pleading look distinguished Cai's anger.

"Okay, but," Cai wagged her index finger at Thad, "if you ever hide anything from me, again, or you screw us over in anyway, I'll come after you myself! Got it?" Thad nodded. "Give me the pendant!" Cai held out her hand.

"But..." Thad pulled it to his chest.

"But nothin', Jack!" Carmen appeared next to Cai. "You want us to trust you, give 'er the necklace. You have to trust us, too!" Carmen tilted her chin toward Neka.

"John gave this to me and told me to keep it safe. I'm not giving it up to anyone! I have nothing to hide from you!" Neka palmed the necklace and shoved it in her pocket.

Simon leaned toward Thad and jokingly asked,

"Apparently Carmen has this thing about some guy named Jack."

Thad laughed, lightening the mood, but a sharp look from Carmen cut off his chuckle.

"Wait! I wonder, since that's John's pendant, if it will work for you?" Nathan crossed his arms over his chest.

"I don't know. I don't even know what it could do for me. He said he was taking a big risk giving it to me. They would find out about him, or he couldn't hide or something like that. I don't even know what it does."

"Try this: keep the necklace in your hand just like that and think about John. Get an image of him in your mind." Jaz concentrated on Neka.

"Okay. Should I like, close my eyes or something?"

"Just think something about him. See him."

Neka closed her eyes, not because she had to, but because she wanted to. She wanted to see John's face.

"Sheez! Somebody has the hots for that guy!" Jaz shook his head. "Stop! Apparently, those pendants are designed for the owner."

"So it doesn't work for you." Cai turned to Thad, "Hand it over. The point is we keep these safe from him, since we now know he is searching for them. One of us will hold onto them each day, no one person two days in row. He must never find these necklaces." Cai cringed at the rising danger of their situation.

"I have a better idea," Nathan stepped to the center of the room. "We'll need a clean knife."

"No!" The others argued, knowing his plan.

"But they'll never find them," Nathan opened his arms wide. "Just remove them from the chain and cut me open."

"No! That puts all the danger on you. And what if I get caught by them? I can't shield my identity, my power." Thad chimed in.

"He already knows who we are, who you are. He knows what we're capable of. He knows we're all here, too, according to John." Neka glanced around the ceiling, her suspicion alerted. *How did he know?*

"So there's another reason he wants them. We need to get them out of this house," Cheater thought.

One by one, the teens filtered to the back door.

Rebecca tucked Maive's note into her pocket.

Cautiously, Jaz twisted the knob and pulled the back door open.

A hooded figure stood beyond the screen and Jaz slammed the door, locking it, leaning his back into it. *"Too late!"*

The screen door squeaked.

Jaz felt a light tap at the center of his back through the wood door.

"Neka! Neka! Are you there? Open the door," a faint whisper called.

"Who is that? Nashota?" Cai's silent question brought a shake of Neka's head, "It's John!"

"Are you sure?" Cai demanded blocking Neka's reach for the knob.

"Yes, it's me, John. The force already knows about me. *He* knows about the faction within the force, too. We're safer together than apart right now. Let me in, please. Hurry, before..."

Jaz pulled the door open and stood behind it, a look of concern on his face as the others waited. The Gifted Ones joined hands as John moved through the screen door.

"Cute." John nodded as he entered, "Look," John pushed the hood back from his face, closed the door and reached out with his left hand to block Jaz while Neka reached for John's right hand to bring him into the blend.

The twelve of them filled the kitchen again, huddled around the back door. Neka threw her arms around John. Blood rushed to his face and out of embarrassment he patted her back, pushing her gently away. *"Let's get outta the house! Fast!"* John silently communicated to the others.

They moved quickly through the post midnight air, the importance of the day trumped by the urgency of the moment.

141

The clock had just struck one minute into December twenty-fourth.

An eerie silence followed the group through the pastures. The wee hour caused a memory to resurface as Neka moved silently over the ground.

Neka rubbed her eyes when the hall light filtered through her door. Nashota's silhouette cast a shadow into her bedroom. "What are you doing? Close the door!" Neka waved him off. She was up late the night before at a sleepover. All she wanted to do right now was sleep...

"Dad sent me to wake you up," Nashota pushed the door all the way open. "Come on! Hurry!"

"Is he ever going to stop moving us around? We're teenagers already. Can we just have a life?" Neka buried her head under the pillow blocking out the light and her brother's words.

"Neka!" Her dad's firm whisper called from the bottom of the stairwell. "Get up, now!"

"Rrrr!" Neka spat as she sat up and threw her pillow at Nashota. "Coming!" she replied.

"Get dressed. Dad told me we have to leave now." Nashota vanished from the doorway. Neka shook her head. After her mom was murdered, her

dad had devised an emergency plan of escape. Neka pulled on her clothes as quickly as possible, thinking how her dad had grown so paranoid since her mother's death. Why did he even have this stupid plan in place?

Neka heard the rustling downstairs. The townhouse where they currently lived had paper thin walls. Nobody lived next-door though. However, if a real threat stood near this drafty old townhouse, they probably heard the entire exchange.

Neka raised her window. The plan was to split up on exit and meet at a prearranged destination. Quietly, Neka slipped out the window to the roof. She reached back under the open window to lower it as far down as she could. To an intruder, it would appear the window had been opened for fresh air.

Neka sat on the roof and counted. Then, she moved close to the oak tree that hung over the edge of the roof and grabbed the branch. Working her hands down the thick branch to the trunk, she swung her legs out to grasp the trunk. From there, she worked her way down every branch until she was able to slip down to the ground.

"Don't look back; just keep running!" Her father's instructions replayed in her mind. But she did stop and look back, once when she heard the loud noise from the area of the townhouses and all she saw was an orange glow on the horizon as sirens filled the *midnight hour.*

When she arrived at the meeting location, Nashota was the only one that showed up. The police picked them up on a curfew violation, found out they lived in the townhouse, and told them of their father's fate.

Two days later, Neka went to the foster home, and Nashota found her. They'd been on their own since.

Neka swallowed a lump forming in her throat. Now is not the time to cry, she told herself. Then she felt a comforting hand on her shoulder. She knew the touch. She turned to smile at her brother, but what she really wanted was to cry on his shoulder.

"It's the last place to look. He has to be here with the others. We've searched all over town." The driver drummed the steering wheel with his fingertips.

"Yeah, it's likely he is, but he also knows the danger it would put on the rest of the Gifted Ones. He's smart enough to know not to come here, to the farm." *At least I hope he is,* the passenger thought.

"Well, this is where he wanted to meet up!" A quick glance in the rearview mirror revealed the other vehicles in wait. "Our job is to go up to the door like we're investigating a complaint and see if we can spot him. We know what he looks like. We've read all their files."

"Yes, so you should know that might not work. One of them can do that thing, you know, disappear or whatever. They'll just hide from us." The passenger looked over his shoulder at the cars waiting for word. "We better do something soon, though. His car will arrive any minute."

"Right. All we can do is try. I'd rather go in easy than blow in the door like a tornado. We're liable to wind up in one if we do that." The driver's jaw tensed over fear of a run in with the Gifted Ones.

"Yeah, you mean because of tornado boy? Can you imagine growing up with a kid like that? Whew!" He kept the conversation going, stalling as well. He felt certain the twelve were already in route, but he wanted to make sure.

"But you know, the one girl? She has no powers. Maybe we can snatch her. Make her tell us where the nephew is. He could use her as leverage, maybe." The driver suggested.

You have absolutely no clue why we're here, the passenger thought. They'd been lied to, all of them— made to think the twelve teens were murderers, thieves, evil souls... like *him.* His followers had been fed so much propaganda about these kids that the troops were either fearful of contact or driven to kill on sight. "Okay, let's go check."

Each opened his door.

"All units hold until *he* arrives."

"10-4, Boss." The Captain's relieved reply filled the first car.

Quietly, thankfully, both officers returned to their seats and closed their doors.

"Here it is!" Cai pulled the makeshift door away and stepped inside. "Last one in seals off that opening!" She nodded as Nathan put the fake door back in place. "We'd best not talk or make a sound. If you hear anything, keep silent. If the seal comes down, blend. You know where you belong. Except John, yours should be near mine."

Each found their location beneath the spiral and when John closed in on his light and took the final position, the spiral lit the dark interior.

"What happens now?" John asked.

"I don't know." Cai responded. They'd all hoped that John was the missing piece. They were running out of time.

"That's it?"

Patient eyes remained on the ceiling.

"It must be activated another way. We're missing something." Carmen searched the interior.

"Maybe 'something' isn't right. Technically,

there's thirteen of us. Maybe it's someone, like Neka's brother? Maybe the number in the fairytale was wrong." Rebecca offered.

Neka stepped away and her place in the spiral went dark.

The truth, Mom? What is the truth you want me to tell them?

"Where's the flashlight? No point keeping this thing lit up while we think this through. It'll just make it easier to get caught. Let's take a look at that letter from Maive. Maybe she knows something we don't." Rebecca pulled the envelope from her pocket as Carmen lit the flashlight in the corner farthest from the spiral.

"If not, then we should try bringing our mothers to us. They may be the missing connection."

"Who is this Maive, anyway?" Carmen's rounded eyes rolled with surprise by her newfound communication ability. Wow! She mouthed.

"A good person we met, a friend. That's her car in the garage. She's trustworthy." Nathan nodded.

Rebecca handed the note to Carmen, but Carmen forced the light and note into Cai's hands, still unsure of her new ability and untrusting of those around her.

"'My Dear Friends,

My time is coming. I will likely be gone before you read this. Miss Dee and her family will be cared for, as will you all. Contact them if you need anything.

There is a faction formed among the force who wishes to destroy you and our world. You may already know this, but a young man, John will come to you," Cai paused and they all glanced at him. *"He is one of the faction and you can trust him because he is also one of you. We of the faction were positioned in places of power — and unlikely places along the way— to guide you, to protect and serve the mission of the Gifted Ones. That's why we knew your story. John's uncle is the one who orchestrated your lives, your futures, your powers. He is the one behind the master plan for this world, but your mothers were wise enough to recognize the change in him, his desires, and they began a stand against his plan. There are twelve of you, no matter what you currently know or want to believe; there are only twelve as the story tells.*

If you haven't figured it out yet, you are only half of this world, a hybrid of sorts. The one who seeks to destroy you is not of this world... he is not one of us. Not all you've been told, or will be told, is untrue, though. Hold tight to each other and stay strong in the mission. Trust yourselves, your intuitions. Be strong.

I know this letter won't answer all your questions, or perhaps even make much sense, and there is much I don't know about the prophecy as I am only the treasurer of your future.

If you can get to the faction, they can help you, but only as far as they can. If you can communicate with them, they know what you will need to complete the mission your mothers began— and gave their lives for— and the faction may point you toward your answers.

I hope you've found the final destination, the place where your dream, or nightmare, will become reality. Your mission will be completed there, but only through the prophecy, the truth, and that is something none of us know. Many have been blinded, but the faction has been working on a plan to help you. Only you will be able to fulfill this mission, though. By now, given the date, the end is close. Be cautious who you trust.

Take care, my children.

Remember me when the mission is complete! It should now be close to your special day.

My deepest love and gratitude,

Maive'"

"Again, with the truth!" Neka broke the vow of silent communication with a frustrated outburst. Something, a memory, hugged her consciousness, barely visible as she closed her eyes.

"Neka!" John warned sternly.

Moments of alert listening followed.

"Remember her when the mission is complete? I will always remember her. She's one of the few people in this life who didn't see me as abnormal." A tear dropped from Rebecca's cheek.

"I didn't know her, but you know we can see her again, so don't let this sway our focus. When she mentioned the day, I remembered something else, it's..." Simon began.

"...our birthdays." They all finished in unison. Nathan clamped his hand on Simon's shoulder in a final attempt to heal Simon's confused mind. He'd

tried several times since Simon's arrival, and each attempt returned more memories to Simon.

Smiles lit the dark outbuilding. *This should be a day of celebration for us all,* Cheater glanced around the circle.

We can celebrate when we take down that miserable excuse for a..." Thad added.

"*John, who is in the faction? Do you know anyone we can contact?*" Lena leaned over John as if to make her silent question reach his ears easier. She hadn't grasped the ease of her new telepathic abilities, either.

"*Considering my uncle is searching for me, and the faction only sends encrypted messages with the dispatcher, I have no idea who is in the faction anymore. One of his top assistants used to be, but I'm not sure if he still is. It would be impossible to reach him even if I knew for sure he was. We don't have a headquarters. We don't meet due to the risk of being caught. And, some that we thought were part of the faction turned to his side. He's very persuasive from what I've heard and seen.*"

"*You've never met him?*" Neka touched his forearm.

"*No, I've only seen him in my... nightmares.*" John answered. "*And just like you, he killed my parents, his own brother and sister-in-law.*"

"*I'm so sorry,*" Cheater empathized with the

hurt in his face and reached across the space between them to touch his arm.

"Man! I just want to grab him by the throat and watch the life..." Nathan stopped, realizing now was not the time for so much anger.

"How are we supposed to get in touch with any of them if we don't know for sure who is and who isn't?"

"Shh! Did you hear that? Outside?" Curious frowns turned toward the opening while some smirked at the irony of Cai's warning. All attention focused on the noise outside the building.

U nable to locate the nephew— or any of the others — within the house, the patrol spread over the property to search outbuildings. They'd been over the property a hundred times without success in locating the spiral.

In the backseat of the limousine, memories haunted the man whose vision for the world opposed that written years ago. Ancestry led him here, provided everything he would need, to finally acquire that which his lineage desired most, but then the prophecy came.

The prophecy predicted the twelve, their use of the spiral to balance the energy shift that entered the earth all those years ago when one being found his way to the planet and made one decision that forever disrupted the balance. He smiled at the memory of that one evil action, passed down to him and committed to his thoughts in such a way— through the dagger of memory— that he believed himself the evildoer from the past.

A warning had been sent. Again, he remembered it as though it were meant specifically for him. That very parchment scroll now resided among his family treasures until this moment. It came to the world, to the people, yet few saw it before the prophecy vanished. Those few believers had caused many problems for his ancestors, for him, along the way. Yet, they were able to persuade the majority of the population that it was just another fantasy tale construed by one person who harbored a wild imagination and the storytelling skills to create a world that would be devoured by a monster. It was just another fairytale. There was no need for the planet to worry over this fairytale, be alarmed by the outcome. That in fact, if such a tale were true, it would be the twelve who would harm the planet, for how could one man do so much harm? And slowly, the people believed in the darkness that fell now over three quarters of the planet. From there, it was easy to make the Gifted Ones the target of evil that now blanketed the earth.

The planet was new then, when he... well, his ancestor landed. It had been reborn yet, again. At that time, the first man and woman in the luxurious garden had been the oldest story refreshed and retold through the generations, even older than the fairytale.

He knew all the old stories passed down through the years, but others never caught on with the followers like this one did, and those other stories eventually died away, went untold—but not the Book of Truth. That book was still touted as the one guide to living happily, peacefully; its histories, its prophecies, its stories were told in many forms, languages, under varying titles. But who authored the Book of Truth? Who inspired its wisdom? Who brought these twelve powers of the universe together? Who wrote the prophecy that would soon be fulfilled by his own hands?

This world of ignorant beings knew the Book of Truth to be the book they longed for and needed, but it had been easy to sway the majority to hate— so very easy. Each continent, each country, each city had their own Book of Truth. Each book told them of their origin. Each book provided rules for them to follow. But his ancestors knew this people would never be happy, for they had a unique disposition, a dual internal spirit of good and evil. There resided a darkness in all of them, no matter how minute. It only needed cultivation— a smothering of the light by his ancestors. His ancestors created division and suspicion in every land by using the various books of truth.

Of course the real Book of Truth, its prophecy, its ideals, were impossible for this people to live by.

Twelve powers could not reside in one innocent world. It was a stupid mistake to plant them all here, in this pitiful world with its pitiful, easily misguided sheep.

He smiled now at the division they had created since the beginning, the evil they had spread over the world, the lies they had told followers from all walks of life. He smiled as he thought of the world today, the number of poor and destitute, the riches he had stolen from powerful individuals who didn't believe the truth, how easily a little riches turned most. He was now the richest man on Earth, a multitude of followers turning to him for the promise of their own riches, a lie of course. He would see that his home, this Earth, became the only power of the universe, that the wealth of each planet, each solar system, each galaxy would become his alone. He would own the natural resources in each by the hands of the followers and slaves he would rule.

He had been one of the first to orchestrate the habitation of this planet. Smart, charming, persuasive and powerful, he climbed each rung on the ladder of leaders until he now stood in such a place of power as to see his ideas, his desires, fulfilled. But his desires would never be enough. The author of the prophecy predicted his greed would be his end. Of course he would change that, and it would be the end of all things good and fair and just in this world and those beyond.

His unfulfilled desire to rule all universes filled him with rage directed at the teens he now sought. When his plans went awry years ago, when those horrid women volunteered to host... Well, he had taken care of most of them already. Damn those women and their deceitfulness! He sneered as he thought of each one, the last one still alive and awaiting her precisely timed death.

He hoped the patrols listened. They needn't harm a hair on any of those spawns of betrayal until he arrived. He had the only devices that could transfer their powers to him, but first he had to rid them of the last two protective devices.

He knew how to take their lives, each and every one. He knew the weaknesses of each Gifted One and how to rid this world of them, even Nathan, the one who could heal. His weakness was simple. This was coveted information passed down to him from his ancestors. They knew because they had rid the universe of twelve royals so many years ago, or so it was written.

When it came to the end, he would finally have what he needed to gain Earth's precious powerful resources and rule all! He knew everything about each of them, except how to gain all of their powers in this one confrontation. This guidance would come to him with the dagger's edge during their torture.

He watched on his seat mounted tablet— fed by each patrol leader's hat cam— as his skilled patrol moved quickly through the vast farm, quietly pausing at each building in futile attempts to hear anything within. He saw the shadows move around, in and out. The Gifted Ones were here on the farm. Where else could they go? It was the prophecy.

"Boss, I think I heard something over here!" The radio crackled into the center of the backseat of the limo.

What did I say about using the radio? An almost immediate text from his tablet.

Anger rose in the backseat as the monster checked his GPS to pinpoint the location of the disobedient officer and he texted the mapped image to the patrol. He would be dealt with silently later.

He only hoped John was here and not in hiding somewhere in the city. He needed him here for the final accumulation of power. He was, after all, a descendent. He opened his car door.

An officer nodded as the first in command approached him. Scanning the exterior, the officer moved slowly around the building. No openings appeared until his eyes focused on the location of a sound coming from near the floor of the building. His pace quickened, and he motioned for the others. The FIC waited, the tension rising as his own boss, the one who would move up the ladder should this mission fail, eased up behind him.

There at the bottom of the wall was a slight curve in the earth where dirt had been carved out to make way for a crawl space. The patrol surrounded the opening as the noise within grew more urgent.

Something, someone, was moving closer to the bottom of the wall.

"It's the only way to find the faction. I have to get caught." John shrugged. "I'm going out." John moved to the

"No! There has to be another way. Nashota! Nobody will see him. He hides well. He won't get caught!" Neka offered.

"Speaking of your brother, where is he? Why haven't we seen him?" Carmen's suspicion rose.

Concerned eyes turned to Neka whose confusion dulled her vibrant features in the darkness. They didn't believe her that Nashota was there. Why did he have to be so...? Where was he now, when she needed him the most?

"Perhaps the traitor is Nashota?" Nathan asked. "Maybe that is the truth your mom wants you to remember."

"No! Nashota is my twin. He is good at heart, not evil. He wouldn't betray us. We know each other very well. But, maybe it is a traitor that keeps the *spiral from working,"* Neka argued.

Was there still a traitor among them?

All eyes turned toward Thad. Cautious distrust filled them. Was it possible the spiral didn't work because Thad was the traitor? Could he block the spiral?

"Cheater, we need to talk to our mothers. We're turning against each other, which is probably what that monster wants us to do. Have you thought of a way we can bring them all here without exerting so much energy?" Rebecca's quiet voice filled their minds.

"No, but I'll take the risk and try to bring eleven of them here. I think I can; I mean, it's my thing, right?" Cheater volunteered.

"The problem is not your power, it's what it does to you. What if it's too much and you don't have the energy for what is coming afterward? I don't like the idea," Jaz warned. *"There must be a way to reach all of them without draining energy from those who change."*

An exterior noise followed by pursuing silence had set them all on edge. The tension of the coming confrontation made them jumpy. Was there someone lurking? Who was it? What were they doing out there? Would the fiery dream come to fruition now before they were ready?

John stepped silently to the hidden opening.

He picked up a board they had leaned against the wall and raised it like a bat.

Neka's eyes pleaded with John as the board rested on his shoulder beneath the crackling moon light. *"We need their help,"* John tore pained eyes from Neka as he readied for the coming fight near the makeshift door.

The handgun held steady at the opening, but a tremor passed beneath the skin of the well-trained officer handling the weapon.

Not knowing which of the Gifted Ones might emerge, the officer's life flashed briefly before his eyes. His seven year old son, his nine month old son, his beautiful wife, their lives threatened by his very action in the next second.

He could die right now, by the hand of a Gifted One. And because his wife had disagreed with his choice to provide a better life for them by following this path, staying with the force, she would be next at the hands of the same man who wanted the twelve teens dead for the sake of power. If she knew that she was his reason for staying with the force, that her life had been threatened by him, she would run with the boys. But she didn't know, and the next few seconds of his life could determine her fate as well as his.

What would happen to his sons then?

Forcing the thoughts from his mind, he waited while the rustling beyond the wall drew closer.

The officer raised a finger to his lips and pointed at the opening as the monster silently watched on the large tablet connected to the limo, his back tense with anticipation.

Whoever was inside that building was about to emerge.

The officer pictured his family, a mental portrait of happiness. The tremor within his body grew stronger, and he relaxed his trigger finger slightly to avoid a misfire.

His family... they were his everything. They were the reason why he signed up for this job, this search— well their protection was the reason. He really didn't believe in the cause, but he had to protect his family.

He didn't want to kill anyone, especially not a kid, but these kids were dangerous beings. Weren't they? That's what he told them all.

These kids had the potential to...

The officer blinked away sweat droplets trailing from his forehead as he steadied himself.

He was too young to die.

W *as that fur? White fur?*

What kind of trick was this?

What were those kids doing in there?

The two officers shrugged at each other as they watched what appeared to be a rabbit's tail poking through the hole.

A rabbit was making all that noise?

The officer closest to the hole raised an eyebrow in the Chief's direction and shook his head. Curiosity brought his vision back to the rabbit butt that now appeared. The back legs were motionless.

The officer gave the wait signal watching intently. The rabbit wasn't making it's own way out the opening. It was being pushed outward by a white speckled— snout?

Two paws appeared, one on either side of the snout, as the dog squeezed between the barn wall and the U shaped dirt.

"A damn dog!" The officer feigned disgust, but a

sigh of relief escaped his nostrils. He almost laughed.

Splash's head appeared. His eyes widened at the sight of the officers. "Ruff!" The dog warned. Then he released a loud growl, snarl, and snap. He grabbed his prey and pulled it back into the barn.

"It was just a dog." The officer moved away from the gap and around the corner where once alone, he leaned relieved shoulders against the worn wood.

Perhaps he wasn't going to die today after all.

The sedan eased up to the farm's location, and the monster sneered in the backseat.

They are here, he told himself.

"*S plash! That was a warning bark! He saw
something threatening! Have they surrounded the
property? Are they everywhere?*" Rebecca slipped
back into the darkness toward the spiral.

Others followed her lead. Was *he* here, the
monster they were to battle? Was it time to end the
fairytale?

Neka remained in place watching John as he
listened intently to the noises on the other side of the
wall. "*I have to go!*"

"John?" A whisper filtered through the cracked
wall. "John? Are you in there? If you are, stay there.
I'll clear this..."

John kept the board raised. Neka placed a
hand gently on John's forearm to stop him from
running out.

"Did you hear something over here?" The
gruffness in the voice overpowered the whispered
words.

"No. No, I was just confirming there's nothing in this building, either. Tagging it now!"

A whooshing sound, as if a vandal were spraying paint made the teens focus more intently.

"Unh! Let's move onto the next one. Too many stinking places to hide on this property."

John silently returned the board to the dirt before his feet. Neka's tender touch firmed to a grip on John's arm as she steered him away from the opening. The group huddled in the darkest corner, farthest from the opening, waiting for silence beyond the walls.

No thoughts.

No whispers.

No motions.

A heightened sense of evil filtered through the barn into their bodies causing their neck hairs to rise, forcing them to blend in the darkness.

Was the monster that close to their location?

Could he sense fear?

If so, he would know they were in that barn as he approached.

A dimmed light shined toward the opening.

"They're here. I feel them. They are still on this property," The monster growled.

"Sir, not this building, it's been tagged. I haven't seen anything. Nobody has. Except for that dog."

"If I had been there sooner, I would have ripped that dog's head off! Give me that flashlight!" Twelve hands gripped tighter as the next beam shone near them. "They've been here. They've been in this building. I sense them."

"Searching for the spiral, sir?"

"Mhm, perhaps. Looking for the one thing that might help them. I want bulldozers. End of day, today. I want every building on this property flattened to the ground before midnight. They die before the end of this day!"

"But, sir, the neighbors..."

"Well, if anyone shows up here, we'll take care of them. Won't we? I'm sure you can think of something clever to tell them."

"Uhm, yessir." The assistant nodded.

"Let's go. Give the order for the dozers. I want this farm brought to the ground."

"Now sir? Nobody will be awake now. The City isn't even..."

"Now! I don't care! Call their homes! Wake them up! I own the Mayor! And before everyone leaves this property, I want that house searched for the last two amulets!"

With little time to waste, the twelve maintained their position until the silence was so deafening they could no longer stand it. They couldn't be seen, but they couldn't risk being caught. They now had two problems to solve without returning to the house: Contacting their mothers and keeping the spiral intact.

Why wasn't the spiral working?

The dim barn interior warmed slightly as the sun rose in the eastern sky. Trying to hold the blend, Jaz lifted his shoulder to wipe his brow, but a droplet escaped to his eye bringing a temporary sting. He blinked, curbed the thought he almost shared, and finally closed his eyes going with the sting. He was finding it difficult to not check in on his new family, though he could feel Cheater's and Cai's hands wrapped around his own. As if in response to his concern, Cheater squeezed his hand lightly. Though they knew their powers worked without touching now, they found comfort in the simple act of holding hands.

"Everyone's left..." The whisper was so quiet they almost missed it beneath the whistling breeze that began at sunrise. Tension gripped them as light shown through the opening they created, then dissolved, again. "I know you're here, John. It's okay now."

John broke the blend and rose to his feet. In seconds he greeted the visitor with hugs and pats on the back. He hadn't seen him since joining the force. "It's good to see you, man!"

"Same! Thought I'd never see you, again. Good

hiding, there, just like the old days." The other man nodded.

"How'd you know I was here?" John asked.

The man smiled and shook his head. "I always knew where you were, man! You couldn't hide from me."

"True dat! Hey, guys, it's okay. You can show yourselves. I want you to meet my brother, well, adopted brother. He's here to help."

Reluctantly, each of them let go of the blend. John trusted this man, but could they?

"Zeke," John smiled and nodded to them.

"So, is this it? This the one we need to keep the dozer away from?" He patted the barn wall scanning the interior, but nothing appeared out of the ordinary. Just another old barn.

John glanced back at the others finding uncertainty and doubt. Sensing their fear of betrayal, Zeke sighed, "Whew, there for a minute, I thought he was onto me. Thought I was a dead man, bro! He drew his gun and everything. But worse, I thought I gave you guys up. That guy is freakin' psycho!" Zeke shook his head.

"Huh, yeah. I'm just glad I didn't have to grow up around him!" John clapped Zeke's shoulder, "The best place I could've wound up was right there with your family after the circle."

"I hear ya'."

Leaving his hand on Zeke's shoulder, John turned to the others, noting their distrust had diminished. "Yeah, this is it. If the faction can keep them away from this barn until last, that would be great.

"Well, he said demolish everything. That might be difficult," Nathan joined them. "Sounded like when he said everything, he meant it. We can't let him do that. That's my grandparents' house. I can't let him destroy this place!" Anger built in Nathan. His fists clenched. He wanted to kill this guy, whoever he was.

"Hold on, hold on. Calm down, Nathan. Nothing's happening, yet. If you two are on the force, how come you act like you haven't seen each other in a long time?" Cai eyed each of them in the silence.

"We haven't," John's confident answer confused them all. "He's a little higher up than I am, aren't ya' bro?"

"Uh, yeah, just a little." Zeke shyly admitted.

"Yeah, like, third in command. I'm just like, getting started. Well, was... I'm definitely not gonna miss that gig! Psycho would be an understatement. I saw too much violence on that fo..." John stopped, realizing what he almost admitted.

Zeke noted the look in his friend's eyes, "Right. I just want this to be over. So this is the crew," Zeke changed the subject. "It's a pleasure to assist you in your mission. If there's one thing about our

176

childhood that I remember, it's your mother's fairytale that you told me a gazillion times! To think it was true," Smiling, he shook his head in disbelief. Before him, beside him, they stood, the Gifted Ones. "Immediate needs? I gotta scram before *he* realizes I'm not around, but I can send somebody trustworthy back with necessities. Here, take this," he handed John a phone. "It's a burner. The number's pre programmed. If I text you, you'll know it's me. Don't answer anyone else. Text me a list of needs. Hide out here as long as you possibly can."

"We shouldn't need anything, do we?" John glanced around.

"Speak for yourself. I'm already starving!" Thad added. Laughter surrounded John and Zeke.

"I guess some food would be nice. We'll be here until we figure this out, until the mission is complete," Cai added.

"Gone without food plenty of times before now. We may not have time for anything but the mission, whatever that is." Carmen's firm response set the room a buzz as Zeke left through the opening. "I'll send Brandy out with some supplies. She'll leave them at the opening. I'll go back and hold off the dozers off as long as I can. If anything changes, I'll text you."

"Thanks, man!" John shook his friend's hand.

"Let's get to work," Cai clapped her hands

together and eagerly nodded.

Knowing they could communicate with their mothers was much easier than the act of communicating with them. After several failed attempts, they determined one or more of them must perform the transfer. Something was holding them back, keeping the transformation from happening.

Or, could it be their mothers were holding them back?

But why?

Returning to the spiral, they watched as the lights glowed above them, each light circling, a spiral within the spiral, each teen rotated in sync with their light, searching for... anything.

Nothing but millions of tiny spiraling lights.

Simon, hands on his hips moved out of the spiral and stood alone. In deep contemplation, he paced staring at the dirt beneath his feet, his head shaking from side to side. Something was wrong. He could feel it deep inside.

Finally his head snapped up, he returned to the spiral, to the team, and sighed, "I would give just about anything to see my mother again, talk to her, hear her voice through the whisper of wind chimes as she told me the story. I would give anything!" He peered at Jamie. "Me, too," Jamie nodded. "Ditto," Jaz added. Nathan agreed, as did Thad and John.

"I haven't seen my mother in so long that her face is fading from my memories," Lena prompted. "Missing her will never go away." A tear trickled down her cheek as her eyes searched the walls and ceiling, embarrassed to cry in front of her new friends.

"Don't worry, Lena. Sometimes I think I'll forget, too." Cai comforted. "And I," Cheater added. "Put me on that list, too," Rebecca nodded. Neka swallowed hard to quench the tears that might conquer her tough resolve before she choked out, "I will always miss my mother. Always," her words trailed into the stillness of the barn.

Downward cast eyes turned to Carmen after moments of silence. She was the only one who hadn't spoken, not that it seemed to help the situation.

"Why you staring at me? Stop it!" Carmen turned away, stepping from her place in the spiral.

"Carmen?" Simon reached for her shoulder, but she spun away before his touch landed. "Leave me alone!"

"Carmen, what's wrong?" Cheater moved to her

side.

"Why can't you all just leave me alone?" She moved farther away, toward the opening as if to run.

"Carmen don't! If they catch you, we're finished. Our mission, or whatever, is over. The world will stay this way, or worse. Come back, tell us what's bothering you!" Cai pleaded.

"I know what's bothering her!" Jaz offered.

"No you don't!" Carmen whipped around, targeting Jaz with a chilling stare.

"Yeah, I do. You're angry. You're angry at your mother. It doesn't take a mind reader to realize that. But why? You need to fess up. Don't you see? *You* might be the one holding us back from talking to our mothers, getting answers. You're the one who painted this rosy picture for everyone else to see. You. So, out the truth, girl."

"You don't know anything!" Hot tears flooded Carmen's cheeks as she stomped to the darkest corner of the barn.

Simon gripped her elbow before the knuckles of her right hand kissed the old wood of the interior wall. "If you do that, this thing might fall down around us." His breath brushed the top of her head and her neck rolled from side to side in anguish. "She didn't have to leave," Carmen sobbed. "She didn't have to leave *me*," chin to chest, her shoulders shook violently as her anger expelled in hot tears.

181

Eyes glistening with unshed tears, the others huddled behind her, around her. Simon pulled her to him, a brotherly embrace and comforting shoulder. Soon the others embraced them both, holding back tears of empathy.

When Carmen's sobs quieted, through ragged breaths, she explained that her mother had stormed away after a heated argument with her father, never to return, even after her father's fatal accident a month later. Her mother was presumed dead, too. But worse than that, she could see her mother, in her mind, now. No matter how hard she tried, she couldn't cast her mother from her mind.

"It's okay Carmen. We all have memories of our mother, see their faces. Once you let go, her image may start to fade, like ours have, but you'll always remember her." Cai wiped a tear from her own cheek.

"No, that's not what I mean. I know where she is. I can see where she is right now. I can find anybody if I focus on them. I know exactly what she's doing this very minute."

"Wait, you mean you're like, psychically connected or something?"

"Something like that. Once I touch someone, their energy transfers to me. I can use that energy to locate them, like GPS, and I can see them. And that's not all... my intuition is guided by colors. I see the color of the soul or something. There's so much blackness surrounding my mother, us…"

"Wow!" Rang several voices in unison.

"Why did we not know this? Where is your mother, Carmen?" Simon cocked his head to peer down at her.

"In a cage somewhere, like a jail cell, chained to a chair, shackled to the floor. She's hurt. She's trying to be strong, but she cries when nobody's around. I just feel so…"

"Your mother's alive?" Cheater moved closer.

"That's why we can't bring them all here! But still, we should be able to bring the other eleven, shouldn't we?"

"Can you see a location that might help us find your mother?" Nathan puffed out his chest, ready to rescue the only mother they had left between them.

The barrage of questions was too much for Carmen. She pushed her way through them, the tears returning, "You don't get it! I don't care about her. I don't want to help her!" Hands fisted, she turned away from them and fell to her knees in anguish, "I hate her!" A weak statement punctuated by sobs of broken words.

Simon lowered himself to the barn floor in front of Carmen and crossed his legs. "Are you sure about that? Because the way I see it, you wouldn't be so upset about her situation if you hated her."

"She left us!" Carmen screeched, burying her

face in her hands.

Simon brought his palms up, placed them on the sides of her head, and hoped.

Cai approached behind Carmen, but Simon shook his head, brushing her off. Time was running out; Cai spun away in anger. They didn't have time for this self-pity, self-help session. As much as Cai empathized with Carmen, they had a mission. It was going down tonight! Some problems took precedence over others. They needed Carmen, and they needed her now, not later, not after her mother was saved, not after... they needed her now!

John placed a quiet hand on Cai's shoulder causing her to jump. He held out the burner cell so she could read the message.

Does he have a woman held hostage chained in a cage?

Three dots waved for what seemed a lifetime to Cai.

Yes. She's a criminal.

Cai frowned at the words, then looked up at John.

Can you tell me where she is?

John's eyes reflected the waving dots. What was taking so long? Should he tell Zeke the woman was Carmen's mother? John glanced at Cai, peered over his shoulder at Carmen, returned his attention to the screen.

The three dots were gone.

Something happened.

Zeke had to cut off the text stream.

"Besides being one of our mothers, I wonder if she's done something to warrant being chained up like an animal. That's a little excessive!" Cai whispered. John shrugged.

As if Zeke stood in front of them, his response lit the screen, *"She tried to murder him."*

Even the dim lighting couldn't hide their shocked expressions. John's doubt told Cai that scenario was improbable; her even getting close enough to him to attempt a murder couldn't happen. The only way that could happen is if he let her get close, and he would if she was so beautiful that the most basic human parts of him could not resist her. Was she a part of the faction?

John thought about Carmen, again. Maybe that was it. Maybe the boss had been attracted to Carmen's mother.

Can you get a message to her? John typed.

Are you kidding? I'll see what I can do.

Okay, let me know. Thanks!

"Carmen," John moved toward the group huddled around the young girl.

"Do we have to do this now?" Simon protested. "I mean, she's just a kid. She's hurting, John."

In protest, Carmen pushed Simon's hands

from her head and refused his comfort. She wiped her face with the backs of her hands, and protested, "I'm not a kid! Yes, I'm hurting, but so are you, and you, and you, and all of us! Leave me alone!" Standing, she turned away from them all and kicked a pile of old hay. Crossing her arms over her chest, she set her jaw in contemplation.

Simon sighed. It hadn't worked. Would it ever work again? With a touch, with a thought, he used to be able to raise a person's vibrations. Bring them joy through their own memories. "Carmen, we need you, the grown up you. We need you now. You're the one who has to enter the darkness. We need you to work with Cheater... uhm... Sarah and help us. You have to let go of the anger. Trust the help we have on the inside to take care of your mother."

"I don't care about my mother! I pushed her out of my head! I want her out of my life, like she's supposed to be and should be. She left *me*! So, she needs to leave my head, too!" Anger slurred her animated words and the palms of her hands pressed into the sides of her head.

"I can bring one at a time," Cheater shrugged.

"It's too taxing on you. Maybe five of us?" Jaz lifted a shoulder to ear in a half shrug.

"Fine! One of them knows why this is happening, has the answers to the Spiral, the truth of this mission and us, maybe they all do. There's too many 'what-ifs". We need all of them at the same time just in case, and we need Carmen to ask the questions," Simon spoke up, "because her mother is still alive."

Carmen turned to him.

"What?"

"She didn't leave you," Simon began.

So he knows, too? John thought.

"Knows what?" Jaz asked John.

Simon looked Carmen in the eyes. "Your mother was taken. By him..."

"What?" Carmen almost screamed.

"Simon's right, Carmen. How he knows is another problem, but your mom is alive in a cage, chained like an animal. She didn't leave you. I was there, when the force took her. They searched your apartment— trashed it— looking for you, but you were gone." John shook away the shame and turned from them.

"I remember. I was in the car, in the trunk, with her. I didn't know who she was at the time. I thought I was dreaming, because, you know, the concussion thing. I passed out so many times before they threw me out of the car and into the streets. I don't even remember if she was in there the entire time."

Carmen stood up. "She didn't leave me? The spiral on the fridge was her then? I thought it was from my da... You! You were there? You were in my apartment when they took her and you didn't stop them?" She ran at John's back, fists clenched. Jaz— who was first in Carmen's path to John— caught Carmen around the waist and lifted her kicking and screaming body off the floor.

"It was his job, girl! Calm down! He had to do it for the mission!" Jaz struggled to hold her up as she fought the invisible monster in front of her.

"Put me down!" Carmen ordered once she was calm.

"That's why it has to be you, too. Your mom's alive... you can ask the questions. Can you find her?" Cheater touched her shoulder.

"I'll try. Still, I don't know what to ask. I don't know what to do!"

"That's right! You're just a kid." Simon was getting tired of her angry opposition.

"Stop it, Simon!" Carmen moved toward him, fists ready. He wrapped his arms around her, tightening them until she calmed. "Can we count on your help, then?"

Carmen stepped out of Simon's big brother embrace. "How am I supposed to remember everything? How am I supposed to know what to ask them?"

"Here, we'll use the notes on the phone. Each of us will add a question and hope they answer.

Come on!" John ordered.

He opened the notes app and typed the first question.

Come on!" John ordered.

He opened the notes app and typed the first question.

The chained woman looked up when the guard entered. A smirk played across her lips, tainting her beauty with an ugliness the boss would appreciate. "He must have lost them if you're returning. I have nothing to tell you. I don't know where they are. Like every other time you've come to me, nothing. I don't have the power... my daughter does." Her hatred for the officer soured her features as unshed tears stung her eyes. She wouldn't let the tears fall, show her weakness before this idiot, never!

Allowing her head to rest forward, as if weariness had once again taken her spirit, she closed her eyes, tightly forcing back the burn. Mentally talking herself to calmness— all those years of yoga and meditation filling her body and mind— the tension left her shoulders, her back, her arms, limbs that could not completely rest because of the chains. Limp against the cold steel and shackles, she blanked her mind and began to hum.

"Come on, lady! Enough with the new age crap. He's gonna kill you if you don't cooperate." A touch on the officer's shoulder forced him to turn, reach for his weapon. "I'll take it from here," the gruff command reached into her state of unconscious comfort, drawing her from her safe place.

"Yessir."

"That'll be all." The officer nodded toward the steel barred door. He pointed a remote control toward the cameras that surrounded the room, then turned his attention to the woman in the cage.

"Lecia, can you hear me?" He whispered so as not to be heard outside, sympathy punctuating each word.

Silence.

"Lecia?" No answer.

"C'mon, Lecia. Don't play this game with me."

Hmph! Her body jerked in response. She shook her head. "Games? You want to talk about playing games you jack..."

"Stop!" He held up the remote. The pain in his eyes deepened when he saw the new bruise across her left cheek. "Why don't you just cooperate? The kids can handle themselves. They have the powers to do so, Lecia. Please. I didn't mean for this to happen — not to you."

"Aren't you afraid you're going to get caught in here, alone with me? He'll kill you."

"He's not here. Matter of fact, he left me in charge. Most of those who are here right now belong to the faction."

"Then let me go!" She stood as far as the chains would allow. "I need to help her! Help them!"

"Lecia, I can't. How would I explain that to him when he returns?"

"Then kill me. I won't spend another moment with him. His groupies won't touch me again! Kill me, now! That's what is supposed to happen, anyway! Tell him I attacked you. Beat me to death! I don't care!"

"Lecia, you know I can't— won't do that. You know I still..."

"Don't you dare! After everything I've gone through to 'help the mission', don't you dare! If you really loved me, loved your daughter, you would kill me now. Let me go to her in death as is prophesied. Do you know the things he's done to me? The torment I've endured? Please... just kill me now. Better you than anyone else."

"I would rather die than kill you." His pained features at her request had no effect on her own feelings.

"Then let me go and *you* can die." The hate in her eyes cut like a knife in his chest. Tears stung and his features twisted with hurt.

His phone pinged in his pocket breaking the

torment.

Now. Do it now! Clear.

Zeke's timing was impeccable. He couldn't believe the message he read, the fact that he was here, speaking to her right now at this very moment. The fact that they had just talked about this very thing.

Fate did play a part in their lives; this choice was not his.

"Lecia..." he pulled the key ring from his belt as the retractable line zipped her attention to him, "... it's time." He opened the cage door with tears in his eyes. It had been the one thing they argued over, the one thing he never wanted to happen. This, of course, and losing his daughter. He'd joined the faction to keep them alive, but now, here he was, having to fulfill their destinies.

Her head bounced up and a smile almost lifted her lips, her eyes, before she saw his expression. She swallowed hard, tears building.

"You are going to kill me." More a simple statement with the impact of a roar than a question.

"For the mission. Not me. I can't, 'Lecia. If you had only left when I told you to go... taken our girl away..."

She swallowed her words as he keyed open the shackles. How could she leave him, Carmen, at that time? If she had known when she took on this mission all those years ago, she might have said no. If she had known this would be the outcome, she might have refused, but there was the prophecy... and almost sixteen years from conception to death with her daughter. "I love you, sweet Carmen," she whispered. "I know you are angry at me, but in death I will come to you. Please trust that I did not leave you."

"I'll take you out. They will take you to a room, provide a weapon, and when you're ready, you can do what you are supposed to do. I love you." He wrapped his arms around her one last time, kissed her forehead, lips, stared into her eyes.

"For Carmen's world," she nodded. "Let's go. I'm ready."

"**N**o!" Carmen screamed as the others attempted for the third time to bring their late mothers to them.

"Carmen, I know it's not working, but, come on. You can do this." Simon displayed open palms of support in answer to her outburst.

"No, it's not that. I broke through. I can see her, my mom. In chains, but a man just unlocked her. He is moving her. He's leading her to another room. I can't see..."

"What? What's wrong?" Simon placed a hand on Carmen's shoulder. "He took off her chains, gave her a gun, and he turned around... It's my dad! No! No! Mom, stop!

"I haven't had a chance to tell you..." Carmen spoke as if she stood before her mother, then her silence filled the barn as an afternoon Christmas Eve storm rumbled overhead.

"*Carmen?*" Rebecca silently asked.

"She's gone... by her own hand." Like the rain

trickling down the cold steel walls seeking the dry earth, Carmen's tears fell. The only movement from her statuesque body were the tears rolling down her cheeks. "I don't see her anymore, which means..." Her overflowing eyes met Simon's in the dim light.

He pulled her to him in a tight embrace, as a protective brother would a heart broken sister, but this time his tears joined hers.

The loss of their mothers still fractured their hearts each time they remembered, and this time, the memories ripped their hearts in two. Eyes glistened through the barn, tears for Carmen as well as themselves.

Cai sought strength in Jaz, the only two whose eyes remained dry. Anger lit the path of their view and their breaths quickened with each heartbeat. As if every motion in the universe worked against them, both of their spines stiffened against the fight ahead.

How did that monster know we needed her? Cai narrowed her eyes at Jaz. Jaz turned his attention to John, who was already typing into the cell phone.

WTH? They just killed the woman in the cell?

Can't talk now.

The betrayal in John's eyes thickened the

tension in the barn. Zeke was on his side— their side — wasn't he?

Their only hope, their only possible answer for the ending, for instruction, the only mother still alive was gone.

Carmen's guilted grief roared into the thunderous drumming rain that dripped through holes in the roof above them to form dark circles of mud on the earthen floor.

The interior of the barn lit brightly and all eyes turned upward.

"No!" The roar shook the interior of the dark sedan as rain pelted the closed sunroof. "This is not supposed to happen. I'll kill those kids! I swear I'll make each one of them suffer for the delays they've caused me!"

"Sir, none of them controls the weather," Zeke, third assistant in rank, raised a brow at this latest tantrum, eyes watching the torrent of water running down the windshield as it increased in volume.

"Shut up!" The monster violently punched the window of the limo on his right.

Zeke glanced at his phone. "She's gone," he reported to his boss in the back seat.

"Such a waste. Such a beautiful waste. The connection's broken, then? The girl should be devastated, but more importantly, she can't run off to find her mother now as the prophecy stated."

"Yes, you're right, as usual." Inside, a tremor of anger passed through Zeke. He abhorred feeding this monster's ego.

"That should cause a much needed delay. That young lady is emotionally charged. She angers quickly, more so than the others. The lack of truth will keep her in turmoil. It will take time for the others to bring her back around. My timing must be exact."

He glanced down at his expensive gold watch. Another couple of hours and they won't be able to defeat me."

"What about the dozers, Sir?" Zeke swallowed his desire to shoot the man in the back seat and changed the subject.

"What do you think, idiot? They'll be ineffective in this downpour. They've no use to me, now! Cancel them. The girl will seek me out now through the touch of my nephew, and once she does, the connection will work both ways. I'll know exactly which building they're in. Send all the men home. They'll be celebrating great success soon."

"Yessir." Zeke sent a text message. He could almost feel the tension of his brothers in arms in the faction. Had they done enough, provided enough help, guidance?

"You, too. Go!" A grim smile darkened the monster's features. "I'll wait here alone. Nobody can help me fulfill the final part of the prophecy."

"Yessir." *Gladly*, Zeke thought as he opened the

driver's door and popped up the umbrella to block the deluge of icy water seeking his head and shoulders.

Standing with his back to the tinted window, a moment of paranoid fear brought a shiver with a vision of being shot in the back by the man behind him. It passed through his mind, but no shots followed his movement.

He closed his eyes, taking in the sound of the pelting rain, the distant thunder, the water droplets as they raced and puddled. He whispered a desperate prayer while he walked toward the only patrol car left on site.

Pulling open the passenger door, his quiet statement, "Let's go," punctuated by a rumble from the sky overhead thickened the hopelessness within and brought a pained expression from the female officer driving.

"We've done all we can do, Zeke. I brought them enough food to strengthen their bodies. You've provided the information they needed. There's nothing else we can do. They have to do this on their own.

"I love you." Brandy reached across the seat and laid her hand on his arm as she steered the car out the driveway, windshield wipers sweeping frantically at thick rivers of water running down the glass before him. "Whatever happens, I love you," she repeated.

Zeke stared at his hands folded in his lap. Would this be the end, or a new beginning for the world he shared with the woman next to him? He turned his attention to her flawless profile, her intense stare at the road ahead, her perky nose turned up slightly at the end and tightened his hold on her hand. "Ditto," he nodded.

"Where to?" At the stop sign she turned to him, a sad smile turning her lips up at the corners.

"We'll find a place to wait out the rain, but first, let's head over to the station as planned. The force was sent home. It's time for the faction to gather and plan the outcome for the worst case scenario."

"You're the boss." She cast a facetious smile his way, flipped the switch on the emergency lights, and drove toward the station as quickly as the rain allowed.

Inside the barn, the rhythm of the droplets from the roof sped up all around the outside of the lighted area of the spiral.

Darkness settled in the sky behind the thick clouds, but the teens didn't notice.

Zeke had sent a last text of warning to John,

not to touch Carmen, but the phone lay where John dropped it in anger when Zeke didn't answer.

None of the Gifted Ones needed the warning, anyway.

The spiral lighting drew them to their places, feeding their need for knowledge of the future, flashes of memories, pieces of their lives, fitting together in their minds eye.

"Nashota! Nashota, don't run off, please!" Neka reached for her flighty brother. More than anything, she needed his hug, the touch of her twin, and his expression complied. She held tight to him as the spiral brightened above them filling their minds and the room with the purest of golden light, dust particles like glistening glitter swirling with the motion of a globe.

Pain temporarily eased by the spiral's new development, all eyes turned toward Neka, then upward.

John, Cai, Simon, Rebecca, Jamie, N_____, Jaz, Lena, Nathan, Carmen, Thad, Cheater.

Twelve places, eleven names and one letter. Wide eyes searched each other's faces, heads shook, shoulders shrugged, then they turned their attention to Neka.

In the light, sparkles of golden dust shaped itself into a form as they watched. Swirling, quivering golden particles atomizing before their eyes into a boy who held Neka, the twin who previously stood in the place of Neka's empty embrace.

"I remember," Neka sobbed into a golden shoulder.

Two atomized particle hands gripped Neka's shoulders, gently putting distance between her face and his. He nodded once.

"I remembered the truth." A bittersweet smile lifted her damp cheeks.

As they watched, Nashota's form twisted into a speeding spiral of brilliant gold particles. Neka's arms lifted wide at her sides. Her face tipped upward toward the ceiling.

The others could not see her upturned face.

At Neka's end of the spiral, the tiny golden atoms formed a direct line to her heart and dissolved into her chest; rays of light shot from her outward pointing fingertips, from her eyes, ears, mouth.

In mere moments, Nashota was truly gone.

Neka's hands fell to her sides.

Her chin dropped to her chest.

Her knees buckled in weakness from taking in a power she'd never truly owned.

She inhaled several deep, calming breaths and the power her brother had passed to her provided the energy her body needed to rise. Neka turned a sad, determined expression on her peers.

"Mom told us to stay together, forever. I was born first, though she told me it should have been Nashota. I should have been given the power to atomize, but it was really Nashota who was supposed to be the royal... a prince, she said. It was rightfully mine, but twins, Mom said... that's how she explained it to me when I became angry about Nashota being a prince in the story." Neka rambled, her words having little meaning to the others.

She raised her eyes to the barn roof, the shining spiral spreading a golden light on her beautiful features. All eyes followed her gaze and they watched as each letter materialized behind the N, e... k... a.

Neka was now the twelfth... a princess after all.

"But..." John shook his head.

Neka's eyes met his. "Nashota's gone now. Forever. None of you ever saw him because he was never really here. He was only visible to me, sent to protect the power, to protect me, until the moment when we most needed my power. Nashota died with them, with my parents.

"I get it now. I get why he was given the power, the power that he just passed to me so the spiral would be complete, would activate. It was to protect us, the power, from *him*. It was to activate the spiral at just the right time."

John reached for her, pulling her into a tight

embrace, comforting her in this moment of truth.

"Well if that's true, then this, right now, is that moment, the moment of our true mission. We don't even know what's going to happen. We don't know the prophecy!" The desperation in Cai's voice sought explanation from those around her. She glanced at Thad, "But this means, there is no traitor among us." The apology narrowing her eyes met an accepting nod. "Carmen, are you okay? Can you handle it? Are we all ready now to do this not knowing the whole truth, what's going to happen?"

Carmen's angry defiance forced her delicate chin outward, "I'm more than ready. Let's kick this monster's butt!"

She pumped her fist in the air and sought her place in the spiral. Cai nodded, following her lead with the others close behind. John let go of Neka, his hand softly sliding from her shoulder to her delicate, strong fingers as he backed toward his light in the spiral.

Neka hesitated, her name aglow in anticipation of the connection.

It was time. Time to avenge the loss of her closest friend, her parents, all of their families. Time to fulfill the mission that was prophesied in the fairytale without ending.

Were they ready?

Were they strong enough?

Neka moved to the circle of light below her name. The newly powered particles in her body surged as she drew closer, pulses of energy electrifying every nerve below her skin.

Now Neka understood why Nashota had always been so flighty. She wanted to run away herself, the power so strong in her veins.

One more step, one step and the light would join with the particles racing like tiny beetles through her, the power complete. Her central nervous system hyper sensitive, she felt as if she stood naked in the pouring rain unsheltered by the barn's leaky roof. The ray of light lay before her, the spiral lit, ready to do what it was designed to do. Neka suddenly feared the unknown, and she stepped forward as if first learning to walk.

One tiny step into the light.

"Arghhhh!" The roar filled the cab of the sedan as the monster felt the final connection in the spiral take place, calling him to their location. The girl's anger had failed him. He'd known his nephew would tell her about the mother. He'd planned it. "Why didn't that stupid girl attack him?" He beat the front seat with his fists.

She, or maybe another, had been stronger than he thought. The bright light from the barn shot upward pinpointing the location of the spiral.

He didn't need to know where now, though. He'd hoped to find them before the spiral pulled him toward it, desiring a surprise attack on the teens so he could obtain the last amulets. No worries, though. He'd designed a back up plan with the ten amulets he had in his possession.

He let the pull lead him. He had to hurry before...

Throwing the door of the sedan open, the

drenching rain beating against his head and shoulders, he ran to the four wheel drive pick up parked next to the garage.

As if the heavy rain fought against him, delaying his every move— and perhaps it did— he fought back and once inside the four wheel drive truck he raced it onward into the storm, toward the light; rivers of water gaining thickness down the windshield, only temporarily cleared by the wipers as lightning revealed scattered trees in his path.

He skillfully maneuvered the vehicle over slick grassy mud in the pasture, pushed forward through barbed wire fences into the next pasture, and accelerated through the open spaces of plowed fields allowing the spiral's physical connection to him to lead the way.

His determination to reach the barn fed by his fear of the spiral opening.

Everything he had achieved would lay in waste if those teens were successful. The world would know his truth, what he was, where he was from, but there would be no fear from them. The world would know and his plans would be ruined.

His only hope rested in the ten pendants he wore on a chain beneath the tie he now fought to loosen with one hand, while the other hand jerked on the steering wheel as the old truck bounced over ruts and through mud.

He tossed the tie across the cab of the pick up truck, knowing his success— or failure— would mean never having to wear another of those horrid accessories. Ties made him feel collared, and that would never happen again.

Before the monster brought his right hand back to the steering wheel, his fingers gripped the dagger's intricate handle next tucked into his belt and he pulled the blade free, held it to his chest, to the pendants.

The connection of blade to gem surged through him as the two powers fought each other, burning his skin where the pendants lay.

He lay the dagger on the seat, power surging in his veins. Soon it all would be his and he would be rid of these pendants and the juvenile spawn meant to be attached to each one.

The fight of his life lay moments before him, and he would not allow a bunch of children to ruin him, his plans!

He forced the gas pedal to the floor as the wipers pushed ineffectively at the heavy downpour. With each swipe the clearing barely offered a view of the ground lit before him. As the headlights cut through the dark, as the wipers swept faster, glimpses of farm revealed five feet ahead of the truck lay a draw of rushing water.

The deep rushing water in the draw almost stalled the four wheel drive as the monster pushed the vehicle through it, but he mastered the dangerous twists and turns the storm threw his way.

He knew exactly what he would do.

He could see the rays of light growing stronger, closer, bursting high through the cracks in the barn's walls and roof, reaching through the storm as he neared.

Power surged through him as the truck stopped next to the barn, the rain beating fiercely against his face as he jumped out the door; large cold drops like knuckles pelted his face and shoulders doing nothing to sway his actions. The hard rain only angered him more.

He had to reach that opening, stop them before...

Lightning struck so closely that the ground beneath his feet shook forcing him to misstep and fall face first into the mud before him.

"Get up you cursed shell!" He roared. The restrictions of his human form made his mental to physical commands impossible at times. He couldn't wait to rule in his natural form and shed the skin and bones of man, but he wanted to use that facet of himself during the battle.

Nothing could stop him, not the storm, not those teens, not even their mothers!

He pushed to his feet and ran, the deepening golden rays cutting through the downpour, gloating their success as he rounded the corner and spotted the fake door.

He felt the vibration of the spiral before his hand touched the hundred year old wood siding.

His fingers pushed through a crack and he stripped away the makeshift door, flinging it through the storm with abnormal strength.

The spiral on the ceiling rotated, first slowly, then with increasing speed.

"He's here!" Cheater felt the blanket of hatred before the wall to her left opened and a blast of cold, wet wind blew in with the fury of the visitor.

"Don't listen to anything he says!" Thad's fear of his dream behavior lidded his eyes as he remembered his first encounter with that anger, shuttering his eyes provided him false courage.

"The light gave us away! We're not ready! We don't even know what to do!" Carmen's desperate words filled the barn.

"Hands!" The magnetic pull to join hands at that moment was so strong that none needed to hear that one word command from Cai.

Power surged through each body as they reached for the ones on either side of them. Something bigger than they ever imagined— ever experienced— was taking place as they connected, something incredible!

Thad reached timidly for Cheater's left hand, feeling the strange new power this lighted anchor brought him. Yet, wary of the unknown, he struggled against the magnetic pull; his flight sense attempted to take over.

As their fingertips touched, the dark man burst through the gaping hole in the wall. His thunderous voice cried, "Stop! Don't do this! You don't understand what you are doing! We can become the most powerful planet in the universe... the most powerful royalty anywhere."

Thad trembled with fear... fear of whatever awaited their connection, fear of this man, his words, fear for his life, and who he truly was. Thad wanted so desperately to hide behind the teardrop pendant.

"Don't let him feel your fear!" Cheater yelled above the roaring spiral as the dynamic pull forced their hands together.

"Thad! Look at me now!" Cai ordered.

"Dude, we need you! Come on!" Nathan yelled.

Then it happened. The man reached out toward them, trembling in the power he harnessed. Fire shot upward between the Gifted Ones filling the spiral, blocking their view of each other's faces. The flames reached upward to the roof of the barn seeking the wood rafters harboring the spiral.

Then, he was there, right in front of Thad,

within the spiral, but it wasn't a man's face at all, it was a monster, a familiar monster. Thad had seen this face before, but when he opened his eyes again, it was the face of an angry man.

"I made you!" His glare burned into Thad's eyes. "You are mine! Wind and fire."

Flames danced and stretched seeking the Gifted Ones. Angry red flames licked the air before their faces, reached for their hair.

"*Thad!*" Rebecca called out in desperation as the hot flames lifted her hair. Her body rose swiftly and the heated wind made it difficult for her to maintain her grip on the others.

Not Rebecca!

Thad glared into the fierce red eyes. It was their dream come to life. No face... the red eyes. The dream that ended the fairytale they knew so well.

Thad glanced through the flames as Rebecca cried out, the pull on her shoulders as she rose causing her pain. Thad lowered his chin, closed his eyes, and produced his own wind...

"Yes! Feed the flames my boy," the monster breathed into Thad's face.

The tornado Thad produced fought the flaming wind, forcing Rebecca downward.

The monster reached beneath his human clothes producing a small item and the dagger. "How dare you betray me! Betray your own people!" The hot breath yelled against Thads cheek.

"No matter! I will take care of you, as soon as I do away with her," A reptilian smile and the man disappeared from Thad's view.

Locating a large flat stone, the monster turned the stone over, lay a pendant on the flat side, and roared, "Watch as she dies!"

With the dagger in both hands poised over the ungodly head, the monster brought the dagger down with such strength, such force, that the pendant crumbled.

A hate filled laugh echoed over the roar of flames, over the rotation of the spiral in the barn, riding the golden light high above the teens as Rebecca's head fell forward, her body now pulling downward on the arms of those holding her in place. Her grip fell limp in Jamie's and Simon's hands.

"Rebecca! No!" Nathan cried out as anger twisted his features. He watched Rebecca's body weaken before him, and he roared in pain as he tried with all his strength to break the magnetic seal of the hands in his.

"Hold on to her!" Simon yelled hoarsely to Jamie as the flames forced him to roll his head to the side away from them.

The fire made it difficult for Simon to catch his breath. He had to do something fast. He needed her slippery grip to stabilize the magnetic hold, or he needed to move his hand upward, to her wrist, to keep her in place.

This is different from the dream, Jaz thought. *Stay connected!*

We're trying, ten voices struggled to respond.

This creature, this monstrous man, held more power than the teens imagined.

You won't win, the man's voice filled their heads.

Through the flames they sought each other's eyes for strength.

The monster now had access to Rebecca's power.

The powerful being knew the crumbled amulet's effect would not last as he threatened to force the dagger into another of the teens amulets, but did the eleven teens know?

Amulet dangling and a rag-doll like Rebecca hanging in the flames' upwind, the man approached Thad again. "This one could be yours, or..."

Thad turned from the horrid, twisted face breathing down on him. His eyes caught Cheater's pleading ones. She shook her head.

"Or maybe... hers?" The monster grinned toward Cheater, a throaty, threatening laugh bubbling upward from stomach to his esophagus and out through jagged, reptilian teeth.

Cheater winced at the appearance of the monster. His features now were much worse than anything she had imagined when she attempted to fill in the face. But now she knew why the billboard on the side of the road creeped her out. Now she knew that face was the face missing in her nightmare.

Turning from Cheater, he moved among the

Gifted Teens, around before them. Inside the maze-like spiral, he kept his distance, sniffing each teen as if smelling fear. Stopping at Lena, he looked up into her downturned face. Her eyes were closed in concentration as her height brought her strain while gripping the hands of the two others.

"You," he said, "are next, unless..."

"Any other time, I'd squash you like the reptile you are!" Lena growled.

Her wide eyed counterparts sent her a look of surprise having never seen her exhibit anger.

Suddenly Lena's own eyes widened as she watched the man levitate to meet her gaze and face her.

How?

He peered deep into Lena's wide, blue eyes searching... for what?

"You don't know the truth." He paused, turned an ear to the entrance where a low grumble forced his attention, then he circled back to face Cheater.

He had been so close to making his way to the center.

"Do any of you know the truth?" He bellowed in her face in Cheater's face, his hot, smelly breath burning her nostrils, but she had seen so much in her short life that his threatening action only strengthened her resolve against him, against the evil. She challenged the monster with upturned chin

226

and soulful eyes.

There was no changing him, though. She knew that before she tried, but she still had to study his face for a weakness. The evil within him only built her courage.

"You do know that your pitiful little power won't sway me, don't you? I don't care about anyone from my past, living or dead!" The monster bared his fang like teeth. "By the way, that little boy, Thomas? That's correct, isn't it? The one you thought was your long lost brother?" Cheater sensed the monster was about to reveal something she didn't want to hear, something that would destroy her resolve.

"Don't listen to him," John squeezed her hand tighter to turn her attention away from him.

"That sweet little boy... oh, and that cute little doggy!" The monster's face presented as a loving father while he shook his head. "Well, that sweet boy is gone now. That little doggy was a tasty one!" He snarled; the whispered words tugged at Cheater's heart, but it was his next move that almost made her break the bond.

The monster flung Splash back through the hole in the wall with such force and flame that Cheater swore she heard a sound like Splash's dying whimper over the rumbling storm.

John and Thad could feel Cheater's grip loosen. It was the first time Cheater showed anger since any of them had met her. She was their rock, their guide on a better path, a gentler path. They never thought she would become angry, never prepared her for such a response.

Cheater had always been the stable one.

"A nice tender snack I'll save for my win. Now... where was I?" The man's index finger tapped his chin. "Oh yes! You don't know the truth about your mother, do you?" His face centimeters from Cheater's own, he angled it left, then right, studying her eyes. Stroking her cheek with the top of his index fingernail, he whispered, "I know the truth. Do you want to know the truth about your mother, why all of those horrible things happened to you? Why all those people you loved died? Do you want to know your truth, sweet Sarah?"

Cheater tried not to blink against his threat, but she couldn't stop herself. He used her only hope, her mother's love, to tempt her into the evil world he'd created, the evil he spun now. This monster was offering to give her the very piece of information she came to Paradise to learn... the truth, but what did her mother, her hope, have to do with the truth, the deaths, the world she lived in?

Why would he point the blame at her mother?

As if reading her mind, he smiled, his dark eyes close enough to her own that she could see flecks of red spike and rise within the shiny black irises. The flames between her and this creature reflected in those eyes, the red responding to the dancing flames.

He's not human, Cheater thought squinting to refocus her attention on one hypnotizing eye, away from the horrible words he spoke. The corners of the creature's eyes turned upward in a smile of acknowledgement that grew with her contemplation of this new piece of the puzzle. "That's right, sweet Sarah. You are correct. You win the door prize!"

He whirled with joy at her discovery and bellowed with contempt, "That's right!" He clapped. "I am not human!" He roared as he spun away from Cheater.

With fierceness and folly he spun with levitating force around the outside of the spiral in a sprint of success. With each circle, the hot wind built forcing the teens to recognize a similarity.

"No!" Thad yelled, closing his eyes against the flames, against the truth.

"He's trying to trick us. Don't listen to him!" Cai yelled.

"Ohohohohoho!" The floating monster threw back his head, then stopped suddenly before John. "You, my nephew, forsook me. I would be hurt, if it were possible for me to feel pain, but it was prophesied that one would turn against me, one would become a traitor. Would you like to see it? The prophecy? I have it, you know? And I have prepared against it.

"You. Your betrayal. You would be next, if I had your amulet." And with that outburst he zoomed back to the rock on the floor. "Alas, I do have hers!" He feigned a distraught look at Neka, lowered her amulet to the rock, raised the dagger above his head, and thrust it into the amulet.

Neka fell silent, her head bent in death.

"No!" John struggled, pulling against the magnetism between the teens. He wanted his hands around the monster's neck. He wouldn't even acknowledge that this creature, this evil being from some ungodly destination, related to him or his family in any way.

John had seen so much pain, so much destruction, so much hatred. He'd heard of the prophecy, through the ranks, searched for it as a member of the faction, but without success— and now he lived it. Tears of frustration burned in John's eyes; his heart burned with hatred he now felt for this thing tormenting them and the love he might have had with Neka. He'd known— the moment he peered through the crack in the barn siding and spotted her— that she was the one who would share his life with him.

She was like him, would understand his strange behavior, his powers, and she won his heart with a look. He wanted to keep her safe, but he couldn't... just like his parents, his sister. His anger grew as this horrid monster returned to face him, a satisfied look in his eyes.

John's nostrils flared. His urge to let go and fight this thing before him, one on one pulled against the magnetic restraints keeping him in the spiral.

"Yes... that's it nephew... that's it. You can do it. Just hate me enough..." the monster whispered, his fowl breath falling on John's cheek.

"John, I know you want to hate him, but don't! You're buying into his plan. Stop what you are feeling right now! Think of the mission!" Cai yelled toward him. John's face turned to her in an attempt to break the mental connection.

Cai was right, and if he had to die to save the world, at least he would be with Neka forever.

"Is that what you think, my little one, my boy, my prodigy?" The hot whisper reached into John's right ear. "You think you will be with that girl forever in some afterlife?"

"Don't listen! Tune him out!" Cheater yelled over the roaring flames. "He's using your emotional connection. Don't let him!" John heard Cheater's request over the flames, felt the surge of energy his friends sent through their connection, and he closed his mind to the face , to the words, coming from beside him. In his mind's eye, he saw Cheater, her resolve, her strength through all she suffered. How was it this girl could endure so much in her life and be so strong against this monster?

"How, indeed?" The monster frowned in curiosity and stroked John's cheek with a creepy fingernail, then he dissolved in a flurry of atoms, and regrouped to face Cheater. "How energizing! To be able to fly apart and together again. That poor, sweet girl..." he smiled up at the churning spiral, two lights out.

"I'm saving you for last, sweet Sarah. Do you want to know why?" He tempted her.

Cheater remained silent, emotionless, like a statue in a park. She faced him without a flinch.

"Oh, my dearest, the last for last. There is a darkness in you that runs so deep. All I have to do to force it to come out is... Well, perhaps I should save that bit of juiciness. I'll give you a little clue as a gift: Stephan. Happy birthday, my sweet, solemn, darling." Cheater felt the hot lips on her forehead and cringed. The warm perspiring fingers on her cheek lingered, but she hadn't closed her eyes against them. She stopped the rush of thoughts— memories — from surfacing, pushed away the flashes with such force that she surprised even herself.

"Very nice!" The man nodded, his brows raising in surprise. "Your mother taught you well. I may keep you around a while after this night has passed." He nodded.

The monster's left hand rose and Neka's body followed the motion as the hot force of flame threatened the grips of Jaz and Jamie. Both of Jamie's arms now struggled to stay connected. Jamie felt as if his shoulders were being pulled from their sockets as one of his feet struggled to remain on the ground, the toe of his shoe just touching the aged dirt below.

Distraction, Thad thought as his body vibrated with fear. The fiery wind changed direction and pushed the flames downward as Thad fell into a deep concentration. Neka and Rebecca returned to the ground forced down by Thad's wind of determination.

Cai wanted to blend them, but she knew the effort would be fruitless. They had to stay in the spiral, keep it going. The magnetism of the spiral's force kept them in place.

This creature wanted to stop the spiral, stop the teens from doing whatever it was that this spiral was sent here to do. She couldn't think of a way that blending with the flames could help them. It was the first time in her life that she felt her gift was worthless to her. With that feeling, the monster appeared, his face before hers.

"Yes, that's right! Your power is worthless. Poor, Cai. You could all blend... hide, go ahead! But I will know because of this magnificently frightening spiral. But please, do blend! Try, for daddy. Shut down the spiral for me. Go ahead."

"Shut up!" Cai yelled back. His goading infuriated her! Her helplessness dissipated as her anger grew.

"Yes! Yes!" The monster clapped, grinning from ear to ear and shaking with anticipation. Cai felt the pain in her left hand as John squeezed her fingers harder. The much needed pain was a reminder of the mission. The pain served its purpose as Cai broke the connection with her anger. She turned a silent thank you to John.

The monster dangled her amulet before her. "You know, I could use that anger of yours later. I'm going to spare you, too."

That was his second mistake.

He returned to the rock with a different amulet, sending a wink toward Carmen.

"Colors are so important in the world today, aren't they? White— pretty much a useless color in a box of crayons, but life? Black— so dark and foreboding, downright scary, right darling Carmen? Yes, so many more colors to see; red— a strong foundation; orange — creativity; yellow—focused, isn't that how it goes Carmen? Green for love? Do you love... Carmen? Do you see green when you peer through the flames at me? Tell, me, what color do you see?" With that last question, he crumbled the third amulet with the dagger and the remaining nine Gifted Ones turned to see Jamie's head slump forward. Three in a row of their friends now sagged, held up only by Simon, Jaz and the winds of Thad.

"No!" Lena cried out. "Not Batman! I'll pound you if I get the chance you... you..."

"Oh, my! Batman hadn't even come into his true power yet, silly girl. If he had, he would have sent for more help. He was worthless to you all, but of course, he had purpose for me. His built in sonar will be useful to reach the outer limits before I shut down this disturbing machine you so conveniently gathered to activate.

"Yes, it seems I've awakened the gentle giant, Lena, by taking her friend's life. Such mean things to say to a nice man like me! Imagine me, able to grow to immeasurable heights! Did you know you could do that dear Lena? Did you know that you were genetically modified to grow at will? So why have you stopped where you are, my dear?" He cradled her chin in one hand and shook it gently side to side. She growled in response.

"Ugh! I don't have time for you right now. Two of you have something I want. You know who you are, and I'm sure by now, you know what *those items* are. I'll bet one of them is you." He atomized to appear in front of Thad, again.

Don't listen to him, Thad! We will beat him even without... without the fallen. Cai sent him the message.

"That's right. Don't listen, Thad. Just because I made you who you are doesn't give me the right to threaten you," the monster mocked.

"You didn't make me who I am! My mother did!" Thad tightened his hand on Cheater's, but flames grew up between them. He peered through the flames squeezing tightly, crying out as the flames licked at his wrist.

As fire creates wind, the twelve, still fully connected, rotated within the spiral with the fire the was forced back in the whirlwind Thad had created. High above the stranger's angry words, high above the seeking flames, both man and wind turned in the center of the spiral pushing back the flames as they rose higher and higher.

"Ha! You think you can beat me, but you can't. Not without your mothers' protective pendants. And as I kill each of you off, I'll know where to look for the last two!"

Doubt filled their faces because they knew two couldn't beat him.

They felt the downward pull as the monster's power lowered them slightly toward the flames, the belief of heat growing beneath them.

"No! Don't listen to him, Thad!" Cai screamed above the roar.

"Focus!" Simon yelled through the challenging wind and flame, pulling at Rebecca's lifeless body to stay connected. If he could just let go long enough to hold her head in his hands, he might...

"I see. Now I see how ungrateful you all are that I gave you every power you have!"

The monster moved to the rock.

Is that true? Cai reached out to John. If anyone would know it would be him.

"Of course, it's true, Cai! Ask me! He wouldn't

know. He was just a sparkle in the test tube's glass when he was modified for his special power. Have you figured out who saved your life that night, my brilliant nephew?

"One by one, you will all fall."

The time was closing in on the creature of fire. He had to hurry. Time was stolen with every turn of the spiral, and he still needed the last two amulets.

"You gave us nothing! All you did was take everything away!" Cheater challenged.

"Oh, poor little Sarah." He pouted, "Stop trying to delay me. I'm going to smash another one of you anyway." He laid the next amulet on the rock; it's crystal-like surface reflected the non luminous veil of the flames sending forth dancing prisms; he raised the dagger, and yelled, "Who is next to fall?"

S imon's head slumped forward.

Four in a row.

Four down.

This couldn't be how it ended. There were so many lives at stake. This world, their world, hung in the balance between good and evil, and they hadn't figured out how to defeat him.

How many have to die? Thad thought as he loosed his grip on Carmen's hand.

Cheater held firm to his, gripped it tighter. "No! The fairytale! Remember the royal chant; recite it now, word for word."

"We have to find a way, a different way to defeat him." Carmen told Thad before closing her eyes.

The demonic man moved into Carmen's view, "Oh, dear color seer. So brave. So confident, or is she? Tell me, little Carmen, what color is your mother now?" He tempted the young girl.

"Arrgh!" Carmen growled in response, the noise

beginning low and growing louder than his last words. Quickly switching moods, Carmen quietly began, "We are The Gifted Ones; the royals. We are connected..."

Cheater joined in, "to each other through blood, through right, through distance. We've travelled far and wide to reach this..."

Thad picked up the chant, "...to reach this place, to achieve our mission. Where one touches one we share our powers forever..."

Jaz closed his eyes, remembering as he recited, "...for together we can bring justice to the poor, tame the unruly, reward the unselfish."

Cai spoke louder than the rest, "We will protect what is now, what is past, and what is future."

"Stop!" The command shook the barn, caused the spiral to tremble, and paused the voices, interrupting the Gifted Ones' chant. "Do you know whose blood you are connected by?" The monster ripped through the barn circling them at inhuman speed.

The flames responded to his motion, growing, flickering, and reaching until they were blown back by the words of the chant.

The faster the monster moved the louder the chant grew. The creature paused at the rock, placed another amulet on it's smooth surface, and smashed it with the tip of his dagger.

A deep voice dropped from the chant silencing them all.

Lena was down.

Jaz struggled in the pull of both girls at his sides, both unable to lift their arms. Jaz screeched in pain, begging for help.

Thad inhaled deeply and strengthened his wind to lift Lena. They could hear the relief in Jaz as he continued to chant, "...we are protected from the evil that surges in and around this world, this universe, and beyond."

"Not another word!" The monster's size increased so quickly that he now towered over the teens, his scaly crown close to the barn's rafters overhead. The fear for their not yet fallen friends tugged at each heart; the unknown of the spiral, of their ending, closer than it had ever been to them. Their compassion, their love for all living beings, for each other, for their families, stopped their attempt again as the dragon man returned to the rock, fell to his knees, lifted the dagger, and crumbled Carmen's amulet.

Now he could see them in their glory. He knew who was their foundation. He knew which one would bring them to their knees.

Cheater cried out, "No, Thad! No weakness! Don't let go, please!"

Thad turned desperate eyes to Cheater. How

could he let any of the others go? "We're all dying," he cried, his guilt overtaking him.

The dragon man cocked his head, locating the reddest of those left.

"Where there are two, there are twelve!" Nathan shouted to Thad the ending of the chant reminding him as long as Thad and John were still alive, the twelve were still alive. "Don't let go!"

What will happen to them? The unspoken words crinkled Thad's eyes, burning tears forming.

"Bow to me now, and I will save the rest of you!" The bellow rose above all noise in the barn, the flames licking higher with the tone.

Another amulet crushed beneath the monster's thrust.

Cai's body fell limp.

And the monster was gone.

"No!" Thad screamed. "Not her!" Thad's heart ripped in two. Rage tensed his jaw as his face twisted with hatred. He ground his teeth together and screamed.

He could not see the monster, who now blended with his background. His large reddish, green body now hidden. The Gifted Ones didn't know where he might turn up next, who he would threaten. He now had half their powers and a great advantage over them.

"Yes! Yes! There you are. There's the one I was searching for. You are of my line. Feel that anger, that desire to kill. Feel it!" the whisper blew down upon Thad though he could not see the creature above him.

Thad's eyes burned as the monster's fiery wind sped up; Thad matched it tossing dust and flames, old hay, shards of amulet throughout the barn.

"Oh, perhaps I shouldn't have done that." The

P.G. SHRIVER

monster tapped his index finger to his pursed lips. "But then, if you destroy the others with your power, I won't have to. Please, do continue."

"Thad stop!" Jaz yelled.

"Thad I can't see! Stop before you blind someone!" Cheater squeezed her eyes closed against hair and debris.

The wind slowed. Thad started to relax.

"Oh, I can't wait any longer! You're too annoying! Your strength is only matched by your stupidity, silly girl!" The monster man shook his head at Cheater, returned to the stone, and smashed her amulet.

Thad cried out in pain. The torrent of grief ripping through him at that moment filled the barn with gales of force. The roof of the old barn flew off, leaving only the churning spiral above them. Thad pushed his power so hard that even the rain drops flew back up and away from the opening.

Jaz watched the commotion ahead, the lightning just beyond the spiral streaked the sky with continual bolts spreading above and beyond where the Gifted Ones circled. None had seen a storm of this nature.

We can't predict the end. We must follow our destinies. We must complete this mission, Cai's voice — strong and resolved— filled Thad just as a wall creaked against the tossing and turning within the building. *Put aside your pain, your anger, Thad. We need you.* He heard her plea as tears flowed freely down his cheeks, tears as hot as the flames the monster forced upward. *You have the strength. I believe in you.*

"Cai," Thad sobbed. "Why Cai? Why Rebecca? Why Sarah? Why not me?" Thad challenged the monster. "Break mine!"

"No, Thad! No!" Jaz pulled his eyes from the mesmerizing show above and sought Thad's face as he yelled.

Never let go! Rebecca's voice reminded him.

How many times did they have to sway him? He couldn't be trusted. He wasn't strong enough.

Jaz slumped as the next amulet shattered.

Thad felt the spiral slow, a cog in the wheel of motion. He knew it was Jaz before he even opened his eyes. He was going to kill them all.

One thing that Thad had never been was strong. He wasn't strong enough to deter the monster's intention. He wasn't strong enough...

Nathan fell next.

Two more angry Gifted Ones were down.

Two remained.

Now the monster knew.

"Whatever you do, Thad, don't lose it. Hang on!" John shouted over the roar of wind and flame. "Where there are two, there are twelve!" He reminded

Thad.

"Give them to me!" The monster bellowed.

"No, Uncle, no!" John yelled, the first and last time he would call this thing "uncle".

"You know I'm not really your uncle, right? We are not of the same place, the same... people." His face neared John's, a sneer of satisfaction, a narrowing of his snake-like eyes.

"No doubt." John returned smartly. "I have absolutely no doubt about that. I would never be like you, so we couldn't be related."

"Hmm, I heard from the force that you had a smart tongue," the monster paused before raising the dagger over his head, "Give it to me, now!"

John squinted into the black slitted eyes of the monster. "Go ahead. Do it!"

"You don't believe I will take your life? How arrogant can you be?"

"No, I believe you can't use force against me. That's what you told the force. You know how gossip spreads in the force? Something about a mirror effect?" John narrowed his eyes.

Thad wanted so desperately to let go and check the pulses of those next to him. He couldn't believe it would end like this. All this suffering— caused by this thing— for what? Death? He shook his head as he listened to the exchange between John and this demon. Could he and John save the world? Was it even possible, now? Thad knew how weak he really was. How could he even remotely help John.

The monster disappeared, but the flow of his direction moved the flames, indicating his appearance before Thad. "Your amulet. Where is it? Give it to me, now!" He held out his rough claw, now only hosting three fingers and a thumb.

"I don't know what you're talking about!" Thad yelled back. "I never had one of those things!"

"Oh you are a poor liar..." the monster shook his head.

"Give them to me!" He whirled and ordered, again flames sought both of the last two Gifted Ones standing.

"We don't have them!" John yelled over the commotion. As he turned his face from the striving flames, he noticed the containment of the fire. The barn wasn't burning. *This rotted wood should be ashes, cinder, even in the storm,* he realized.

He faced forward, the flames licking at his skin. There was heat, but no real burn. It had only been their expectation of the fire that brought heat. The monster produced a fire that didn't burn. Was this...

"We're at a stalemate, Thad! Don't give in. He can't touch us. That means..." John yelled over the commotion.

"Shut up! You horrid being. You don't deserve

to protect this grand planet! You're the worm of all the worlds. You..." The monster stopped in front of John.

John smiled in his face. "You... lose," John said calmly.

"This is winning?" The monster spread his arms at the spiral of fallen still rotating.

"He's right! We're not winning, John. Look around!" Thad didn't want to give up, but it seemed there was no other choice. He'd already taken ten of the Gifted Ones. As if he'd snapped a finger and dropped them with the sound. How could they win against powers like that?

To lose is to win, a familiar voice filtered into Thad's mind. He frowned at the words. Was it a memory breaking forth? The wind energy diminished Thad's strength, and though he managed to keep his friends upright, he struggled to push back the flames while keeping up the wind.

"You're growing weaker by the second." The wicked smile faced Thad. "Come now, son. It's time to give up the amulet."

Was Thad delirious? His father's face stared back at him. "Dad?" Thad squinted through the flames.

"That's right, son. Just give him what he wants and you can rest." Thad's dad reached toward him as if to tousle his hair, the way he did when Thad was younger.

"I can't Dad. I can't let go. They need me," Thad shook his head, his eyelids falling closed.

"Sure you can." Thad turned toward John. John seemed to be struggling worse than before as Thad's own power weakened.

To lose is to win, a familiar voice pushed into John's mind. "What? That doesn't make any sense." John argued aloud against the words.

"What doesn't make sense?" the monster questioned. "I know you must be delirious. Your strength is failing you. You both can rest, once you turn over the amulets. You can rest forever with your friends and loved ones. Come now!" The creature held a hand toward John. John worked his dry mouth until he found enough spit to show the monster how he really felt about the request.

"Now, that was just rude!" The monster dried the spittle with a snap of his finger and thumb which brought fire to his face. The fire seemed to suck away the saliva on his features. Then, the creature drew back a claw, ripped off the remaining human skin from its face, and slapped the palm of his talon against his own cheek drawing green blood. When John turned his face toward the monster again, he was looking at a snaky, dragon-like reptilian creature with protruding teeth and flicking forked tongue that now grinned scathingly at him. John's face twisted with disgust, and he turned away from the creature releasing a scream.

To lose is to win, the voice repeated. *Give him the amulet. It is time.*

"No!" John yelled. "I won't let go!" It was some trick, John was sure. With Rebecca's power, the monster could speak telepathically to them.

Thad craned his neck to see what was happening with John, but he couldn't see the monster from that angle.

What was happening? Thad could hear the voice, too.

You don't have to let go of their hands. Just visualize, the voice replied.

Who was sending this message? The voice seemed so familiar to John.

Think! The voice repeated, *To lose is to win.*

John was tired.

Neka was dead.

They were all dead.

He and Thad would be dead soon enough, if not from giving up, then from weakening. They had lost. There was no use. He closed his eyes and saw the amulet in his mind. John envisioned it leaving his pocket to float before his own face.

John opened his eyes and twisting before him on his mother's silver chain, as if supported by air, was his amulet. With each spin, it forced back the flame, an ebb and flow of fire reaching toward it, then blowing away again.

To lose is to win.

T had felt the decline in power as John's amulet splintered before him on the ground.

The reptilian man produced a guttural laugh of pleasure knowing one amulet remained between him and complete control of everything.

One last child, one more royal Gifted One, stood between him and all the powers of the universe.

To lose is to win, the familiarity of the voice tugged at Thad's conscience.

To lose is to win.

To lose is to win.

Is that why John gave up? Is that why they all gave up on him? They wanted to lose. How could it be possible?

In what world did losing mean winning?

They were all dead but Thad. He had been the weakest, the most uncertain, the most untrustworthy of all, and he was the only one left!

"Yes, Thad. Yes, they all left you to deal with

me. You... the weakest. You the most like me. But how could you not be like me? Shed your skin, your human side, and it would be like looking in a mirror. You would look just... like... me!" The reptilian face tilted left to right as its tongue flicked toward Thad.

Thad narrowed his eyes in return. "Is it like looking in a mirror? Really? Somehow, I think I would be better looking, even as a monster. Why? Because I am better than you could ever wish to be! I would never give up on those who believed in me! Never!" Then somewhere in Thad's memories he saw it, he saw what the demon was trying to make them see. "I could never be like you, because you will never have what I have... A position of power in our world, a mother who is human, who gifted me with caring, a purpose that serves others and not myself. No, the mirror wouldn't show me anything similar to you, ever!"

Close your eyes. See the amulet in your pocket. Free it with your mind. Dangle it before him. It was the last act that Thad wanted to fulfill. How long had he been weak? To hold out, to bring his friends back— if he could— would take great strength. He didn't want to give up, now, not on them and not on the mission...

To lose is to win.

Why do you keep saying that? How can I trust you? You might be him! Thad answered.

Let go, Thaddeus.

To lose is to win.

Thad couldn't keep the torrent of wind up any longer. He closed his eyes, visualizing the amulet in his pocket. The chain eased upward, past the opening and the seam, slowly as the struggle to be strong weighed on Thad's conscience.

When Thad opened his eyes, the amulet dangled before them, spinning faster, a light within glowing stronger, a bright, golden light.

"Ah! Yes, I knew you would choose the right path. After all, you are one of mine." The flames grew upward as the monstrous creature's heated words fell against Thad's cheek. The monster snatched the glowing amulet from Thad's view. "But now, you, too, must join your friends as it is written. You should never have been prince."

The creature roared as he prepared the ritual he was given. Visualizing the prophecy scroll, he brought it forth, lay it on the smooth rock, then placed the amulet on top. He positioned the tip of the dagger high above his head. The spiral creaked and whirred in response. He sneered at Thad as he brought the dagger downward.

The spiral of teens slumped to the dirt floor beneath their feet as the creature prepared to take their powers.

The wind inside the barn stopped.

The flames extinguished leaving a dark spiral in the dirt floor.

The twelve teens limply hovered beneath their lighted spaces.

A golden glow encompassed the spiral, the teens, ending at the rock of destruction.

The reptilian being shed every last piece of skin of his human coating, moved to the center of the spiral still whirling slowly above, knelt in the eye, and spread his scaly arms to receive the powers he'd sought for so long. He would soon rule all. He just had to use their powers to press the spiral, open the portal and then...

As the golden energy brightened, an intense beam of light strengthened above the teens casting a blanket like warmth over the them and the creature at the center of the spiral.

Soon, the truth would reveal itself to him; within the whirl, each body glowed as it rose and sped around him, golden light filling the teens' heart spaces, gently working its way out and upward.

Consumed by warmth, as on cue, each Gifted One awakened from the deep darkness they'd been cast into by the destruction of their amulets, a darkness where no stars shined, that no light brightened, a darkness very familiar to Cheater.

Their mothers' forms peered down through the golden light at the center, first upon their children, then upon the man who gave their children life— who modified their human forms to create the beings necessary to protect all that was good— before descending through the opening.

Each mother rested above their child, features filled with sympathy, eyes sparkling with unshed tears, but not for the man at the center; their tears fell for the people whose lives he ruined, the people who lived in poverty and fear, the people free to express their unrighteous acts and anger upon those around them.

Their tears shed for the world they swore to protect.

The spiral slowed and came to a creaking halt.

The sky had opened up beyond the spiral, beyond the storm still raging around the barn at the edges of the gaping hole in the sky.

A brief smile passed between child and mother before all rotated toward the inside of the spiral to face the man at the center. There was no longer a need for the magnetic pull keeping their hands together. Their arms rested at their sides.

"You betrayed us once; you won't again." Cai's mother spoke firmly above her daughter, sadness filling her words over the task that must next be fulfilled. For no good parent wishes to punish their own child, neither does any good being wish to bring death upon another.

"We told you what would happen, all those years ago when we and the council set this plan in motion after the prophecy of ruin." Cheater's mother looked upon the man as though a small, disobedient child crouched before her. Golden fingers rested on her daughter's shoulders as Cheater raised her chin to the spoken words.

"Instead of protection, you have ruined many lives." Rebecca's mom— as soft spoken as her daughter— allowed a tear to escape her chin and fall upon Rebecca's crown. Mistaking it for a sign of forgiveness, the monstrous being glanced up at the twelve beautiful women who circled him. This wasn't the prophecy. This wasn't what was supposed to happen. How could this be?

Gently, the spiraling wind started again, spinning the Gifted Ones and their mothers; the spiral rotated around the alien below them.

This was not the end he desired. Destroying

that prophecy with the last amulet should have brought him transfer.

"It is time," Jaz's mother nodded to those spiraling with her.

"Your greed in this world, your cruel desire for power, determined your own fate." Simon's mother held out her right hand and the others followed her gesture.

Their eyes closed, they turned their golden palms down, and in one motion reassembled the broken pendants, raising them to dangle before the teens so each Gifted One could restore their amulet to their neck. All twelve pendants facing inward of the spiral, formed a shining, softly rotating, prismatic light show above the man.

"No! No! Don't do this! We can rule together!" The man cried out, understanding his defeat and the sentence. He sought their faces above him, his guilt and repentance too late.

Unfolding slowly behind each mother, a set of lightly fluttering, flawless white wings stretched to their maximum capacity filling the walls of the old barn.

The wings flexed not for support, but to pull the man beneath them upward in a united effort; their wings beat, slowly at first, then built speed as a bird uplifting heavy prey in its talons.

The monster's body curled into the fetal position, as if seeking shelter in the egg from which it hatched.

Levitating at their center, the monster spun in circles to the rhythm of the wings, counterclockwise in a prism of light beams, and opposite the spiral's force. The increasing pain-filled knowledge of his fate overtook him and he grimaced, his reptilian features pained.

In unison, the twenty-four powering the spiral spoke as one voice:

"For your rogue decision to serve only yourself

in this Universe, this world— that we sent you to guard for them, for our children and their children and onward— for the lives you chose to take to prosper and support your own plan, for the decision to take all of this and more as your own from its true creator, for your attempt to take the lives of the twelve you helped create in the name of Universal protection, for the Lost Prince, you must spend the rest of your life and beyond in the Darkness.

"No fire shall warm you, no light shall shine upon you, no being shall comfort you. You shall go forth to a darkness so cold, so full of nothingness, that you will find no comfort. A darkness so still you will know no sound, and in its heart, your mind will be lost to this darkness. The remainder of the reptiles you spawned while here will also be cast away into their own darkness, never encountering each other to rise above what will always be, again." As one, their words ended. The spiral gained speed; each mother and child closed their eyes to the creature before them, their minds connected, and they created his forever home.

Within the darkness behind their eyelids, they saw the monster, alone and despondent.

With a flash, their eyes opened and the evil one was gone.

Having cast away the one they entrusted to protect this world from the very thing he would now never escape, mother and child looked at each other, the true test for each of the Gifted Ones about to fall on them.

It had been a difficult decision to trust this one being, to allow him to rise to such power through his political ranks, but they had planned well for an alternative action. As suspected he defied each of them by taking their lives, leaving their twelve children alone and pining for answers. He had helped to bring the life of each child to this earth from their respective planets, provided each life a human host to gain the knowledge and powers of their children upon seeding, and now the answers would come to the teens.

Though the teens believed this to be the end of their story— the end of the fairytale— their journeys had just begun.

With a singular thought, the golden brilliance funneled from each mother as their wings refolded into their backs, and beneath each spiraling light, their own children stood facing them.

The twelve souls descended to the barn floor, standing before their children. Each placed their right hand on the head of their child while covering their child's heart with their left.

The Gifted Ones smiled as the winged mothers spoke:

"These words embed upon your hearts, that

you shall be the protectors of this Earth until the end of time, that you have come unto the end of your fairytale, to begin anew."

"Powers yet not revealed to you, will be revealed."

"You are beauty; you are hope; you are perfection in the Light of all Lights and never shall darkness hide that light or take you over."

"You are the gift, half human, of the twelve reigning planets in the Universe, the princes and princesses sacrificed from their homes to protect this planet."

"You know your world, your power, your Glory, and you shall forever use yourself to fight the fight of these people on this Earth."

"You will remain together, as one, as family, until the end of time."

"When it is time for you to shed your earthly abodes, your children will take your place, as you did ours."

"Your compassion will reign and rebuild."

"Your hearts will fill the lost."

"Your eyes will be opened to the colors of evil."

"You will never be at peace, for haters and evildoers will continue to arise. Mankind can never just be happy. There will always be those who want more."

"You will not need us again to answer

questions, for you only have to ask and you shall know."

"You have proven yourselves worthy of what they will call you... Superheroes of this Earth."

Each teen reached out to their guardians, their mothers, hugging them fiercely, clinging as if to never release them, again. Some, like Sarah, had not felt a mother's touch since the tender early years.

Each mother swiped a right hand over the forehead of her own child passing that golden light into them and with the memories of their truths, their worlds. With delicate hands, they cupped their own child's chin and kissed his or her face before rising as one and dissolving into the spiraling lights above now forming a portal to the beyond.

The spiral creaked to a halt.

The portal closed.

"We did it." Sarah looked around at the others, the hollow words leaving an empty space in her chest. She'd fought to find the truth for so long, leaving behind goodness and kindness wherever she went. What now?

Rebecca took her pendant between finger and thumb, rolling it to watch the golden prism of lights dance inside it. The other eleven followed Rebecca's gesture to move in closer.

Leaving of the lights of their names, the Gifted Ones formed a circle hug beneath the portal, each hand resting upon a shoulder or around a waist, heads tilted back to take in the stars in the dark beyond them, the clouds having parted and cleared the sky above. Smiles lit the twelve faces that had worn sadness for too long.

Splash and the two collies bounced happily through the opening.

"Who's gonna help me fix that roof?" Nathan asked facetiously as he reached down to pat one of the dogs.

"What? No happy birthday? No Merry Christmas? Nothing?" Cheater shook her head at Nathan.

"Back to work as usual... is that all you think about, Jack?" Carmen tossed in. "I mean, we are just teenagers."

"Who is Jack?" Simon feigned frustration.

"Yeah, this will be an interesting bunch to hangout with," Jamie raised a brow toward Rebecca as she scratched Splash's ears and expressed her joy that Splash was okay.

"Oh, come on! Are you two gonna get on that Jack topic, again? I think I can help with the roof, Nathan," Lena offered, raising her hands as if holding up a rafter.

"Hmm, the roof? I wonder where it ended up?" Cai tilted her head in thought.

"Wait! Birthday? That's right, it was yesterday!

What are we having for dinner? I'm starving! Are we gonna have cake?" Thad grinned at the others.

Laughter filled the topless barn, a musical coating of joy that filtered out the open ceiling to flow beyond into the night engulfing the Earth in its light as the golden sun crept slowly up the Eastern horizon on Christmas morning.

Thank you for taking a moment to post your review <u>The Lost Prince</u> at Goodreads and your favorite bookstore here books2read.com/u/4NL6W8.

Enjoy this sneak preview of what I'm working on next

The Hummingbird God

1

$\mathcal{I}$ saw the old, witch woman in the woods.

It was a cliche setting.

Really it was.

How many scary movies begin with some old witch in the woods?

Her long, salt and pepper hair hung past her butt, jutting out over her shoulders in a snarly, tangled mess of dull wire. Planted on her crown was a tattered fishing hat hosting not lures and hooks, but some strange objects I couldn't identify from a distance. She was reaching up, her gnarled, crooked, arthritic fingers bent every which way. I wondered how she could even complete her task with hands like that. A worn, black coat hung on her thin frame down to her ankles. She hadn't noticed me, or at least hadn't acted like she'd noticed me, until I was within her personal space—I was bad about that, getting into a person's personal space, even when ignoring my intuition. After one glance toward me with her rheumy eyes, she continued her work, unbothered by the fact that I watched her so closely.

I should have known when my stomach did that flip.

I should have left her to work and returned home, setting aside my pressing curiosity.

I'd had another argument with my mother, though and—after slamming the back door—ventured off into the woods behind our house to cool down. I guess I walked farther than I'd planned, which tells you how angry I was at her. I could have turned around, humbled myself for an apology, though it would have been fake because Mother was wrong this time. I could have been in my room, but curiosity and compassion became my doom.

I never returned to my room, my home, my mother.

I can't say I've been completely unhappy, because I've found more joy than I ever imagined!

I can't say that I miss my old life entirely, because I found what mother and I argued over the day I left.

Though I've been happier than I would have ever expected, I am imprisoned and now may never break free, but why would my mind feel I needed to?

I may never have a life of simplicity and normalcy.

I may never have the love of my life, the one I desire anyway.

Well, that is unless I decide, or he decides, that love is worth the risk of leaving here.

When I think about the old woman in the woods, I see her as if five minutes have passed since I entered her personal space and asked the simple question, "Would you like some help with that?"

A croaky, harsh chuckle traveled up her throat and escaped her lips before she replied, "Are you sure you want to help?"

"Yes, of course, if you need help. I don't want to offend you."

It was so easy for me to say that simple three letter word then, and now it seems the most difficult word in the English language to pronounce.

"Alrighty!" Her voice crackled, "Take this jug and fill

those." With a sweep of her hand she indicated upside down bottles hanging in the high branches of the trees around us. "It's getting more difficult for me to climb these days."

"What is this?" I took the jug from her hand, a clear, light brown liquid sloshing about inside. I thought it was alcohol.

"Natural sugar water."

"Excuse me? Did you say sugar water?"

"No!" her voice became harsh, "I said natural sugar water! And don't think it anything else!" she turned on me violently. "You heard me the first time! Stop acting stupid, girl! Now, you asked to help, so climb that tree and fill that bottle!"

"Uh... uhm..." Fear knocked at my heart. I wanted to run, but I trembled my way up the tree, with one arm holding the jug. I didn't have to climb the tree the normal way. Someone had driven spikes into it for footholds, and as the tree grew, more spikes were added. At the top, an arm's length from the trunk, hung the bottles. I sat in the tree, lifted a bottle from its hook, and found it screwed into a round cap of some sort, about three inches in diameter, with several tiny holes on its surface, a circular ring around the outside of the cap. "What is this thing?" I called down to the scary, old woman below me.

"Don't you know anything? It's a hummingbird feeder! Again, you act stupid! You cannot help if you are going to be stupid! Stupid will get you in trouble! Stupid will get you exactly ..."

I balanced the round cap on the branch and began filling the bottle, but paused when her words dropped off. Her head flipped sideways, as if receiving a blow from the air. I thought it a tic, some disease crippling her muscles. I knew a little about that.

"Look lady, I just offered to help you. You don't have to be rude. I've never fed a hummingbird before, but I am very smart! I know hummingbirds might be tiny, little birds, but they fly so fast it's hard to see them sometimes. I can learn more, though." I shook my head and finished filling the bottle, replaced it to its perch, and moved down two spikes.

"Oh, you can see them," she whispered. "And they are hungry, greedy, mean little birds. I must keep these jugs filled at all times."

"All times? Don't birds migrate?" I perched on another branch, removing another feeder.

"Of course they do, stupid girl! But these feeders have to be maintained at all times or..." her head whipped to the side again, "We don't get many freezes here. Some of them remain, the older, crotchety ones."

"Uh, I know we don't get freezes often. That's the blight of Texas." I climbed back down the spikes, pausing before going up another tree, "Are you okay?" Tilting my head, and leaning to my right a little didn't provide much of a view of her face. Her hair hung around it and she humbly peered down at her feet as if chastised.

"I'm fine!" The abrupt yell forced me into action. "Just fill the feeders!"

"Okay... okay!" I couldn't wait to get out of there, away from her. She was a horribly bitter person. It was like she didn't enjoy feeding the hummingbirds. If she didn't like doing it, then why do it? I thought hummingbirds were beautiful, delicate creatures. To her, they seemed to be monsters, so why was she doing this? I glanced back down at her. Compared to her, Mom was a cuddly little puppy. This experience would definitely teach me to think before asking to help anyone. "There's only enough left for this feeder, and there's at least..." I did a quick count, "ten more."

"Oh, don't you worry about that. There's plenty more. I'll show you where to fill it when you're finished with that one."

As promised, she led me into the woods a little farther, and there before an old shack, stood a well. A round cover had been placed over the well, and she easily lifted it by a handle from the unhinged side.

Taking the jug from my hand, she hooked it onto the rope and turned the crank until I could no longer see the jug, only the descending rope. Her arthritic fingers jutted out around the handle and she pushed at it with only her palm.Â

As mean as she was, I felt sorry for her, "Would you like me to do that for you?"

"Fine!" she grumbled.

I took over the cranking, the heavy glass jug making it easy to lower. "May I ask you how old you are?"

"You wouldn't believe me if I told you."

I heard a splash below. "Let it go," she said, "wait. I count to 100 and it's full when I pull it up. It'll be heavy!" that deep throated chuckle.

Ugh! It made my spine crawl.

"Why wouldn't I believe you? What, are you like a hundred?"

"Ha! A hundred? Do I look it, then?" her watery, crusty-cornered eyes peered around the well frame at me.

Uh, yeah! I thought, easily. She was starting to creep me out.

"I suppose I should thank you. Ha!"

"Uhm... okay. Never mind." I just wanted to finish the task I volunteered for and leave. The tiny hairs on the back of my neck flickered.

"Go on, then. Pull it up."

She was right. It was quite a bit heavier coming up. I put both hands on the handle and reeled. "Where's the sugar? I suppose in that shack? Can you bring some out?"

"Sugar! Ha!" she cackled, "Stupid, girl!" her head shook back and forth in frustration.

"Stop calling me that! I'm not stupid!" anger made me turn the crank faster. When the jug reached the opening, she pulled it to the side of the well and disconnected the rope. The water was brown.

"Yuck! Are you trying to poison those birds?" I was appalled by the sight of it.

"Pfff! I wish! Now come on, finish up!"

Did she say I wish? She wanted to poison them? I need to get away from her, I told myself, eager to finish the job.

"Aren't you going to add sugar? You're just giving them

this nasty, brown water?" I followed her back to the trees.

"Does it look the same as the other water?"

I peeked around her at the jug. "Yes." I nodded, a bit surprised that I hadn't noticed the color of the water earlier.

"What did I tell you the other was?"

"Sugar water!" I answered, a desire to please her brought a lilt of approval to my voice.

"No! Stupid girl! That's not what I said!" Her biting retort brought an involuntary wince.

Downtrodden, I thought a minute, certain she had said sugar water. "Natural sugar water?" I questioned.

"Ah, not so stupid girl, that is correct." She was sprite for her age and I had a hard time keeping up with her steps. I ran to catch up and reached for the jug. "Seriously? Out of that well? Let me taste it!"

She pulled the jug away, cradled it in one arm and slapped at my greedy hands with her free one. "Never! Never, never, never should you taste this natural sugar water! It is for the birds only! Got it, stupid girl?"

Hmm, back to that again. "Okay, alright, I won't drink it. It's just... It's hard to believe there's natural sugar water in that well. I mean, how's..." I cut the question off. There was no need to hear that I was stupid, again.

I didn't need the answer. I was going to help her and be done with her. I would never return.

Three more trips to the well, alone, and I had finished the job. It was nearly dark by then and I was hungry, tired and eager to return home.

"Well, that does it. I think I'll go home, now."

"No! You can't leave!" She cast a stern look my way, followed by the head turning jerk with which I had become familiar. Her eyes humbled, searching the ground at her feet. "You must be starved. I will get you some dinner and you will behold the fruits of your labor."

"Fruits of my labor? Seriously?" Nobody talks like that anymore. She scurried off to the shack, leaving me to stand among the trees; I glanced up, the multitude of feeders forming a perfect circle around me. The light from the falling rays of sun glinted on the bottles, colorful prisms forming, rays dancing as the bottles moved with the slight breeze. Mesmerized by the jewel-like show it created, I took a seat on one of two tree stumps jutting from the ground, a perfect seat for nature's show. I watched the lights as the bottles and tree limbs moved in time.

"Here!" The old woman shoved a sandwich my way, and then a bottle of pop. I looked at the sandwich, pulling the bread apart. Peanut butter and honey, I could handle that. I hoped I wouldn't have to hear how stupid I was for being a vegetarian. "What? You think I'm stupid? I know you don't eat meat. He wouldn't choose..."

Slap! The noise seemed to come out of thin air. Her head whipped to the side, then her eyes dropped to the ground. "Eat!" The old lady ordered with a jerk of her head.

This woman was definitely weird. I was afraid to eat the sandwich now. I wrapped it up and rose from the stump. "I think

I'll eat it on the way home. I really need to be going now. My mother will be—"

"Wait! Look!" she pointed upward, drawing my attention back to the bottles above.

My eyes followed her crooked finger landing on the most amazing sight I had ever seen.

Hundreds, if not thousands, of tiny birds filled circles around the feeders, landing, drinking, flying away, repeating the process. As I stood there, one tiny, red-throated bird hovered before my eyes, circled my head three times, and returned to hover before me at eye level. It was magical, beautiful, and heartwarming. He zipped away, then rose to the trees to perch near a bottle.

"Sit, watch, and eat your sandwich."

"Okay." There was so much peace in watching the tiny birds that I hardly tasted the sandwich or the root beer.

Through the enchantment of the flight, the feeding, the singing, from another realm I heard her speaking, "I am two hundred and ninety-nine years, eleven months, twenty-nine days, twenty-three hours and forty-nine minutes old. I will be gone before the new hour. You will maintain the feeders from this day forward.

"There's one rule, and one rule only. Remember it: you must not drink the water from the well. Oh, and you may never leave here. He will not allow it, for the feeders must remain full. Your life is now here."

A distant voice, a dreamlike chant, drooping eyes, and

when the birds disappeared at nightfall, the natural sugar water was gone, as well as the old woman whose translucent image wavered as my eyelids closed.

My fifth grade class voted me most likely to be the first woman president of the United States.

My parents expected me to play piano for the New York Philharmonic.

My grandmother thought I would be a star vocalist.

I didn't want any of that. Those were always their dreams for me.

All I ever wanted was to be who I was meant to be.

All I want now is him.

Look for this book and others by this author. Just scan to code below.

About the Author

P. G. SHRIVER lives in Texas with her family of two and four legged beings.

She has been writing since the age of seven and was first published in a local newspaper. Some of her hobbies include gardening, reading, sewing and cooking.

She is a retired Developmental Education instructor and 4-8 teacher. She enjoys writing, traveling and presenting at schools and festivals.

Visit her website today at pgshriver.com! Follow her at

Goodreads: https://www.goodreads.com/author/show/5854923.P_G_Shriver

Facebook: https://www.facebook.com/pgshriverwrites

Instagram: https://www.instagram.com/pgshriverwrites

www.ingramcontent.com/pod-product-compliance
Lightning Source LLC
Chambersburg PA
CBHW011654010726
47499CB00010B/3250